What the critics are saying...

න

"I took much pleasure in following the characters' trains of thoughts and interaction with each other. Their motivations and banter ring so natural and true, I quickly took to Carla, Leo, and Alice as I happily immersed into the book. At the end of the day, I found Carla and Leo well-matched and **Nothing Personal** a cozy tale well worth my time." ~ *All About Romance*

"The story captures the evolution of Leo and Carla's friendship and the realization that the lust is actually love. The characters are personable and fun. I particularly enjoyed the discovery that even though they have known each other for years, Carla and Leo still had to get to know each other on a much deeper level for their relationship to grow." ~ *Fallen Angel Reviews*

"Ms. Adams has penned a heartwarming romance with believable situations and real life complications. This is a steady paced story that grabs the reader from the start and keeps them entertained until the end. This is a wonderful story to curl up with at the end of a long day." ~ *Coffee Time Romance*

ELISA ADAMS

NOTHING PERSONAL

Cerridwen Press

A Cerridwen Press Publication

www.cerridwenpress.com

Nothing Personal

ISBN 9781419954177
ALL RIGHTS RESERVED.
Nothing Personal Copyright © 2005 Elisa Adams
Edited by Martha Punches
Cover art by Syneca

Electronic book Publication August 2005
Trade paperback Publication January 2007

Excerpt from *Grave Silence* Copyright © Elisa Adams 2005

Excerpt from *In Moonlight* Copyright © J.C. Wilder, Liddy Midnight, Elisa Adams 2004

Cerridwen Press is an imprint of Ellora's Cave Publishing, Inc.®

Also by Elisa Adams

෨

Grave Silence
Lost in Suburbia

If you are interested in a spicier read (and are over 18), check out the author's erotic romances at Ellora's Cave Publishing (www.ellorascave.com).

Dark Promises: Demonic Obsession
Dark Promises: Flesh and Blood
Dark Promises: Midnight
Dark Promises: Shift of Fate
Dark Promises: Tarnished
Dirty Pictures
Dream Stalker
Drop Dead Sexy
Eden's Curse
Ellora's Cavemen: Dreams of the Oasis II *(anthology)*
In Darkness
In Moonlight *(anthology)*
Just Another Night

About the Author

&

Born in Gloucester, Massachusetts, Elisa Adams has lived most of her life on the east coast. Formerly a nursing assistant and phlebotomist, writing has been a longtime hobby. Now a full time writer, she lives on the New Hampshire border with three children.

Elisa welcomes comments from readers. You can find her website and email address on her author bio page at www.ellorascave.com or www.cerridwenpress.com.

NOTHING PERSONAL

Chapter One

ഔ

If you had any kind of a life at all, you wouldn't be sitting in your apartment building's laundry room at nearly ten on Friday night. Alone.

Carla rolled her eyes. The thoughts were hers, but the voice in her head sounded suspiciously like her mother's. *Lovely.* "Just what I need. I'm turning into my mother."

"I don't know if that's such a bad thing. Your mother's a great lady."

At the sound of the deep voice behind her, Carla squealed and jumped, almost falling off the dryer she'd been perched on. Her heart stopped for the two seconds it took her mind to register familiarity. "Damn it, Leo. Didn't I warn you about sneaking up on me? How do you always manage to do that?"

He stepped in front of her, an overflowing laundry basket in his arms and his computer bag slung over his shoulder, and gave her a goofy grin. He set the laundry basket on top of a closed washer and placed the computer bag on a nearby chair. His shoulders lifted in a casual shrug, the grin deepening to accentuate the dimple on his left cheek. "What can I say? It's a gift."

She snorted. *Right.* A gift? More like a serious annoyance. Or, it would be if he wasn't so damned sexy. She swallowed. *Knock it off, Carla. He's off limits. So off limits that even looking at him should be illegal.* She scrubbed her hand down her face and shook her head, hoping the motions would bring reality back into focus.

"That's what, a week's worth of laundry you have?"

"Two." He lifted the lid on an empty washing machine and tossed the entire load in, pouring the detergent right from the bottle, without measuring, before he dropped the small, red bottle into the laundry basket, the cap crooked. "I couldn't see my floor, so I thought I should probably clean."

His actions, telltale signs of his bachelorhood, helped ease the sudden jolt of lust. Lust that had, undoubtedly, been caused by staying up late one too many nights this week with black and white movies and pints of ice cream as her only company.

"Are you serious?" She shook her head, trying to keep her jaw from smacking the floor. "This is an apartment building. Where adults live. It isn't a frat house, you know."

What was it with men, anyway? Why did they all assume it was okay to live like pigs as long as there wasn't someone around to tell them different?

He blinked at her, the picture of innocence, before he burst out laughing. "No, I'm not serious. You are *so* easy. I've just been busy with work lately. Laundry's been last on my list, so I've had to wait for the weekends to get it done."

Yeah. *Sure* it had. Men. They were all the same. Putting things off, time and again, until a woman finally stepped in and helped them organize their lives. Maybe he needed to get a maid.

"What are you doing in on Friday night, anyway? Don't you have a hot date?" Didn't he always?

"I had a date, but I'm not sure if I'd classify it as hot." He smiled, shook his head. "We ended the night early and I took her home. No big deal. That's just the way my life has been going lately, you know?"

Anything she'd been about to say floated out of her head as he stripped off his shirt and tossed it into the washing machine. This time, she couldn't do anything to prevent her jaw from dropping, and she wouldn't be surprised if she had drool running down her chin. He must have been *busy* in the gym, for two or three hours every day from the looks of things. She hadn't seen a half naked male body that amazing in too long to remember. An indelicate snort escaped her lips. She hadn't seen a naked male body *at all* in too long to remember. Seeing Leo only served as another reminder that she needed to get out more.

"Um, Leo?" she asked. Or at least she tried to. She couldn't seem to get her voice to a level above a hoarse whisper, and a hot lump had taken up residence in her throat.

If he'd heard her, he didn't let on. He just went about the business of starting the washing machine, oblivious to her sudden inability to breathe. And when he bent over to pick up a sock he'd dropped, gracing her with the perfect view of how those jeans molded his rear, her stomach did some weird fluttery thing. If any other man inspired those sensations in her, she would have been thrilled. Elated. Over the moon. But her best friend's little brother wasn't a man she should be drooling over, no matter how well he'd aged.

Why hadn't she noticed him before, *really* noticed? She'd love to sink her hands into all that thick, dark hair—

Hello! Alice's younger brother!

Right. Get it under control. Get him talking. Listening to him speak about parties and nights out at bars and his endless string of meaningless relationships would remind her of the vast differences between them.

"So, um… H-how's the job?" Nope. Didn't help. Her gaze was still glued to his body and her mind still planted firmly in the gutter. How was she supposed to make idle conversation with the guy when she couldn't form a single coherent thought past the things she'd like to do to him once she had him in her bed?

Which wouldn't be happening. Not in this lifetime.

Come on, Carla. Snap out of it. This was ridiculous. It was *Leo.* She'd known him since he was barely walking. She used to help Alice *baby-sit* him when they'd been in middle school. If that didn't douse her unexpected arousal, she didn't know what would. Being ten years older than the guy, she shouldn't even be *looking* at him much less indulging in the thoughts currently racing through her head. But the thoughts were so tempting. The man was so tempting. *Geez, Carla. You're so weak.*

No. She was so *deprived.* Once she found a man closer to her own age, one who didn't go through women as fast as he changed his socks, she'd forget all about her stupid fantasies.

"Work? It's fine." He dropped the laundry basket onto the ground and moved it aside with a negligent kick. "Hectic, you know?"

Normally, she would have reprimanded him for not taking better care of his possessions, but "normal" didn't come close to describing this encounter. She felt like she'd been sucked into some kind of alternate reality. She had never considered Leo even remotely attractive before tonight.

Liar.

Well, maybe she'd considered it. In passing. But it had been nothing more than a general appreciation of the male form in all its prime-of-life glory. Now, suffering from an acute case of full-blown lust, the sad truth came up and smacked her upside the head.

She needed a man.

Any man would do. It had been *way* too long since she'd had a social life if a *child* like Leo started to look good to her. It had to be a trick of her mind. He couldn't possibly be as sexy as her imagination made him out to be. Could he?

Her IQ dropped a couple of points when he unsnapped the first couple buttons of his fly.

Oh, yes he could.

Before she could catch herself, she let out a soft sigh, which she tried to cover by clearing her throat. Loudly. Several times. "The owners of the building tend to frown on public nudity."

"Do you have firsthand knowledge of that?" He gave her that goofy grin again, the one that should have reminded her why she shouldn't be gawking at him. But it failed. It accentuated his sensual lips, and his perfect white teeth, and the little dimple in his cheek that didn't look so innocent anymore.

She gave herself a mental head slap. *Younger man, Carla! Ten years younger!* Yeah, he was nice to look at, but she couldn't afford to get carried away. She'd just celebrated her thirty-fifth birthday. Way too many candles on the cake to be carrying on about washboard stomachs and well-defined pecs and tight buns that looked great in snug-fitting jeans. At her age, she should be thinking about stable men with great jobs who were interested in settling down and starting a family. Moving into nice, neat little houses in the suburbs and buying minivans. Unfortunately, settling down seemed to be the last thing on her mind at the moment. She wanted to get wild. With Leo.

That is so not going to happen. At least not in this lifetime.

But it didn't hurt to dream.

It took her sluggish mind a few seconds to realize his mouth was moving. He was speaking to her. *Get a grip, Carla. Now.* "Did you say something?"

He laughed. "I asked you how it's going at the salon."

Oh. Work. Why had she been hoping for something other than idle chitchat? Like maybe for him to tell her that she was the sexiest woman he'd ever seen, and he couldn't wait another second to get his hands on her.

She snorted. Yeah, right. Like *that* would ever happen.

"It's great." She attempted a smile, but her numbed facial muscles refused to cooperate. "When is your friend coming in for a haircut?"

Leo's eyes darkened and his jaw tensed. His shoulders stiffened and his easy smile faded. "Cameron?"

What was that about? "Yeah. Cameron. I haven't seen him for a while."

"I'm sure he'll be in soon."

"Good." Was that jealousy she detected in his voice?

One dark eyebrow rose and he crossed his arms over his chest. The position made his pecs bulge even more and she lost her train of thought. The dark look on his usually playful face only added to his appeal. When had he gotten so…grown-up? So sexy that he knocked the breath from her lungs? And why was he so worried about Cameron? She had about as much chance with him as she did with Leo. Maybe even less.

With a shake of his head, Leo turned toward his computer bag and pulled out a small black case. He slipped a pair of thin black wire-framed glasses from the case and put them on. When he turned back to her he smiled, and her stomach clenched into a heated knot. Wow. The small, businesslike frames made him look older, more serious. Sexier. But the spark of mischief had returned to his eyes, and a hint of a grin quirked one corner of his mouth. She swallowed hard. He was perfect. Exactly the type of man she'd always been searching for.

The loud buzz of the dryer under her startled her back to the real world and almost knocked her to the floor. Her clothes were ready, and not a moment too soon. Another few seconds and she might have embarrassed herself by asking him to take her on top of the washing machine.

Yeah, right. Like *that* would ever happen.

She slid off the dryer and yanked the door open, piling her clothes into her little wicker basket before she picked it up and turned around to say goodnight. Once back in the safety of her apartment, she could forget this little lapse in judgment had ever happened and go back to her search for Mr. Right, not Mr. Fantasy. "Well, bye. I guess I'll see you around."

Leo had other ideas. He stepped closer, backing her into the dryer. This was a new development. A little gasp escaped her throat. She clutched her laundry basket tight against her stomach like a shield. The air around them practically crackled and her blood hummed. A sexy, potent smile, very much unlike his trademark grin, curled the corners of his mouth and he leaned toward her as much as the laundry basket separating them would allow. *Oh God.* Her gaze zeroed in on his mouth and her tongue darted out to wet her lips.

He was going to kiss her. And, despite her mind's incessant protests, stopping him wouldn't be an option. Just the thought of those full lips settling over hers had her going all mushy inside. She didn't usually give in to mushiness, and she had no idea how to handle it. Lost and out of her element, she gripped the laundry basket harder, until the wicker bit into her palms. A frisson of panic raced through her. Why hadn't she at least brushed her hair before she left her apartment? She probably looked worse than the Bride of Frankenstein. Well, at least she'd put her toothbrush to good use. If he closed his eyes, the fact that she hadn't washed her face since four a.m. might not bother him.

His fingertips brushed her bare arm, inciting all kinds of riots amongst her touch-starved nerves. They cried out, leapt and jumped toward the heat of his skin. His hand trailed down her side with agonizing slowness until his fingers brushed her hip. A jolt ran through her and she had to fight to remain standing on legs that no longer wanted to hold her upright. His lips hovered just above hers, his warm breath feathering across her skin. His smile turned unbearably sensual, for just a second, before he straightened and backed up a step, a pair of her white granny panties dangling from his long, tanned fingers. His blue eyes sparkled with laughter.

"Here. These were stuck to your shorts."

"My shorts?" She blinked up at him, her mind foggy. What was he talking about? And then his words hit her, along with the urge to sink into the floor and disappear beneath the linoleum. Her face flamed, probably turning cherry red. Could this get any more embarrassing? She scurried for the door, not looking back as she called out, "Well, thanks. I don't know what I would have done if I'd lost my favorite pair."

It wasn't until she'd reached her apartment door a few minutes later that she realized what she'd said. *Oh yes, Stupid. It could definitely get more embarrassing.* She leaned her forehead against the door and replayed the words in her head.

Her favorite pair?

What had she been thinking?

Obviously, not much. The combination of nearly naked male and fabric softener fumes must have disconnected her mind from her mouth. Forget foot-in-mouth disease. She might as well insert her whole leg. It would be a long, *long* time before she could face him again and not imagine him laughing at her choice of undergarments.

She had to try three times before she could get her fingers to stop shaking enough to fit her key into the lock and open the door. When she finally made it inside, she dropped the basket on the beige entryway carpet and rushed into the kitchen for a glass of water to wet her parched throat. She gulped it down and set the glass on the white-tiled counter with a thump. Alice would *kill* her if she knew Carla was fantasizing about all the things she'd like to do to Leo. In her hormonal, baby-on-the-way state, Alice would probably string her up by her toes and let her rot. There was no way she'd approve of Carla doing anything with Leo, let alone everything.

But that knowledge did nothing to stop the fantasies running through her head, waging mutiny on her sex-starved brain.

She groaned and leaned her hip against the counter. She was in deep, sinking further by the second, with no way to stop it from happening.

No. That wasn't true. There was a way. A foolproof one. She couldn't attempt to make good on her fantasies if she never saw him. She'd have to do her best to avoid him from now on.

* * * * *

Leo sat on a cold metal folding chair next to the dryer where Carla had been sitting moments ago, trying to get his mind to focus on the images on his laptop. He had a meeting with a difficult client first thing on Monday morning and a lot of work to prepare beforehand, but with the residual effects of Carla's presence in the room, he couldn't even draw a breath without thinking about her. Funny that he'd all but forgotten about his date with Kelly. His mind had already brushed her aside in favor of Carla.

What she did to him...he couldn't even put it into words. It had always been that way, for as long as he could remember. He'd never found another woman who affected him so strongly. And he'd tried. Maybe a little too hard. But none of them had been able to banish Carla from his mind. What had started out as a childhood crush had only gotten worse with time, and with his moving into the apartment down the hall from hers a few months ago. Living on the top floor of the three-story building, the only things separating their front doors were a few yards of carpeted hallway and dark paneled walls.

Usually he could ignore the pull. He'd been living with it for so long that it had become almost second nature. But tonight his perception on the situation had shifted, giving him a glimmer of hope where before he'd seen none. Fueling his need for her, pushing it to another level.

Carla was interested.

That brought a smile to his face, despite the amount of work he still had left to do before Monday morning. She always brushed off his flirting, treated him like he was still thirteen. A pest, an annoyance she simply tolerated. But tonight, when he'd finally decided to take the next step and try to entice her, he'd seen something different in her eyes. Lust. She hadn't been able to hide it. She wanted him. She'd shown it, and now he had the chance to get exactly what he'd been wanting since he'd first understood what really went on between a woman and a man. He'd be stupid to let an opportunity like this pass him by. More than stupid. If he didn't take full advantage of the situation, he'd never forgive himself.

One question remained. How would he go about getting her where he wanted her, in his bed, in his life, without scaring her off? She'd been skittish tonight, and he didn't want to push her away. But he'd made the right decision, pulling back instead of kissing her like every cell in his body had been aching to do. He had her off balance. Just a little more pushing and she'd topple over.

And he'd be there to catch her fall.

But one thing still bothered him, despite the interest that had been so plain in her gaze. Cameron. She'd asked about him, spoke of the guy like she missed seeing him in the hair salon where she worked. Why was she so curious about Cameron? It ate him up inside to think Carla might have a thing for one of his close friends, but he couldn't discount the possibility. She'd been cutting Cameron's hair for the past year and a half at Leo's recommendation and he'd mentioned his interest in Carla more than once. But Leo had never thought it would be anything more than one-sided. If she was interested in exploring Cameron's attraction to her, it could turn out to be a big problem for Leo and his plans.

Of course, Cameron had no idea how Leo felt about Carla. Not willing to leave himself vulnerable, he had never mentioned his own interest in the woman to anyone. Not even his closest friends, and especially not his family. His mother, his sisters knew, but they'd never made a big deal out of it, so neither had he. Instead he'd pretended it wasn't there. Enjoyed life, enjoyed being young and single and playing the field.

Just like Cameron had. He might be interested in Carla, but he wasn't serious. The guy didn't have it in his genetic makeup. If he did anything to hurt Carla in any way, Leo would take him apart limb by limb, and make sure he felt every excruciating minute.

Shit. "Stop. You're getting so far ahead of yourself you're going to fall behind." He adjusted his glasses and tried to bring his attention back to his work. What was it about Carla that brought out the possessive, jealous jerk inside him? Probably the fact that he'd been half in love with her forever. Reminding himself that he wasn't ready for any kind of long-term commitment didn't help. If he could have Carla, he'd be ready for just about anything. No other woman made him even think about settling down, but Carla… She made him at least consider it. There was something between them, something good, and he refused to go through any more of his life not finding out exactly what that something was.

But how could he convince her to give him a chance? He'd tried being her friend first, and hoping something would develop from that. Obviously it hadn't worked, or he wouldn't be sitting here alone right now. Tonight, he'd tried something new. And if the desire that flashed in her eyes was any indication, it had worked. *That* was his way in. A slow, scorching seduction that would have her jumping into his arms before she even had the chance to protest.

A smile formed on his lips. "Perfect. Absolutely brilliant." He did so love a challenge, and Carla might prove to be his most difficult, and most rewarding, one.

* * * * *

Carla sat on the couch, remote in hand, her gaze glued to yet another old black and white movie on the TV screen. An empty pint-sized carton of ice cream sat on the coffee table, the spoon handle sticking out of it. She should feel guilty for consuming the entire pint in one sitting, but she couldn't bring herself to do it. Her two best sources of therapy were shopping and chocolate, and since it was too late for the mall to be open, chocolate had to do.

Something had changed in the past couple of weeks. A strange kind of restlessness had settled inside her, showing no signs of letting up. Her life had become monotonous, tedious. It was time for a change. But was Leo the change she was looking for? She shook her head. Not likely. Any interest he had in her was a product of her imagination. He had more girlfriends than he knew what to do with. Young ones. Pretty, model-thin ones with blonde hair and big boobs. Ones who, like him, weren't looking for anything beyond the rush of passion, the temporary thrill. She couldn't be that kind of woman. She didn't have it in her to indulge in a casual fling.

Or did she?

Since her strange, exciting laundry room meeting earlier that evening, she'd started considering all kinds of possibilities that had never attracted her before. Most of which included Leo and the toned, sculpted body she'd never noticed before tonight. But it wasn't anything serious. It couldn't be. When she woke up in the morning, she'd be the same Carla Michaels she's always been. Thirty-something hairstylist, serial monogamist.

But, despite all of that, one sad fact remained. She needed to find a man. A man who wanted a normal family life. Given the fact that she'd prefer someone who looked as good as Leo, her chances for finding her Mr. Right were about up there with being the first female president. It all came back to Leo, and what just one look from him could do to her insides. She needed to do something to get him off her mind, but nothing she'd done tonight seemed to be working.

With a sigh of disgust, she switched off the TV and dropped the remote onto the couch cushions, pushing up from her seat and heading toward the bedroom for yet another sleepless night.

Hours later, as she lay flat on her back staring at the ceiling, two things became very clear. If she didn't get some action her body might wither up and die, and she was going to regret that ice cream come morning.

Chapter Two

Ice cream regret came just as she'd expected, in the form of an ultra-intensive, tougher than usual stair climber session at the gym the next morning. Lack of sleep coupled with extensive high fat, high calorie intake, made her morning workout hell on earth. Her muscles were sluggish, and her eyes kept trying to close on their own. Her mind hadn't bothered to wake up yet, and she'd been out of bed for over an hour.

She swiped her hand across her sweaty forehead, picked up her water bottle from the holder and took a deep swig of the ice-cold liquid. It did nothing to ease her parched throat or calm her pounding heart. *Looking decent gets harder and harder with every birthday.*

She snorted at the very idea. In her twenties, workouts had been what she did when she walked from her car to the mall and back again. Calories hadn't even been an issue, and the only wrinkles she saw had been in her clothing. A couple of years ago, she could have eaten an entire gallon of ice cream without an ounce of guilt, or an ounce of excess body fat. Now she spent an hour and a half five days a week doing cardio and lifting weights, all so she could fit into her size eight clothes. Her body refused to drop a single pound, no matter how much she worked at it. But she'd keep showing up at the gym for every session. It was the only way she'd be able to fit into all the outfits she spent a fortune on.

In truth, she was perfectly happy at a size eight, though she worked hard for it. Sometimes too hard. She might not be model-thin—she'd always had a curvy figure, but she hadn't let herself go like a few of her friends from high school and college had.

She sighed. There was a very good reason for that. They were all happily married, with husbands and families, or children on the way. It was sad that, at thirty-five years old, she'd never come close to finding that perfect man. The one who completed her. The one she could grow old with. The one who wouldn't care if a pint of ice cream went straight to her hips or her stomach wasn't as flat as it used to be, no matter how many hundreds of crunches she did to try to control it. One who wouldn't care if she found a few new gray hairs every month and the laugh lines around her eyes seemed to deepen every time she looked in the mirror.

One who was old enough to appreciate the fact that she was aging every day, and women didn't age as gracefully as men. She'd continue to fight the aging process with her regular gym visits, dye jobs, and expensive eye creams, but the sad truth of the matter was that she'd never be able to stop it. She needed a man who would understand that, not one who had been of legal drinking age for only a few years.

Leo, no matter how much he interested her, wasn't the right man for her. At least not the right man for her to marry. But she'd never had a fling before, and the idea had only grown in appeal since the previous night. Though the thought of having her first, and probably only, fling with Leo made her heart skip a couple of beats. Everything about it worried her, but it also gave her a little thrill. She had dinner with his family on a regular basis, since her parents spent most of their time traveling the country. How awkward would that be to sit across from his mother, or worse, Leo and a new girlfriend, and think about what had happened?

And why was she thinking about Leo, anyway? If she was going to do this, she should go all-out. *Definitely not Leo, Carla. Can you say anonymous stranger?* Someone who might actually be interested in her.

She took another long gulp of water from her bottle and wiped away a bead of sweat trailing too close to her eye. Alice had always accused her of thinking too much, of analyzing every situation to death. And she was doing it again. Now wasn't the time to think. It was the time to feel. The time to do, without thought, without regret.

Her session ended and she climbed off, wiped the handlebars with her towel and grabbed her water to head for the showers. She glanced around the gym at the muscle-bound men and perfect women, most younger than her. She really needed to find another gym. One that catered to the middle-aged crowd, or at least those rapidly careening toward that status. One that was populated by professionals, not college students. This one had seemed like a good idea a few years ago, but that was before she'd edged a little closer to forty.

She'd first joined the gym in hopes of finding a man. Those hopes had been dashed, rather quickly, when she first started coming in the mornings and realized with so many perfect blondes with DD cups and IQs almost as high as their shoe sizes, the men had no interest in a thirty-plus redhead with a slightly rounded tummy and pale freckled skin that never tanned. She wasn't ugly, on good days even considered herself fairly attractive, but she wasn't what the gym gods were looking for, either.

If she had to admit the truth, she'd say that none of the men in the gym would excite her in the long run anyway. She'd had a few offers of coffee or dinner, which she knew would have led to one- or two-night stands. In her younger years, casual sex had never interested her. But that was when she'd had a few long-term relationships and had been getting sex on a regular basis. Now, in the middle of the longest dry spell of her adult life, she had to rethink her priorities. She needed a man. Just for a little while. And any man would do. Leo wasn't the only man to have showed a tiny bit of interest in her in the past few years.

She sighed and shook her head. Maybe not, but he was by far the most appealing.

Her gaze landed on one of the personal trainers. Mick? Mike? His name slipped her mind, but over the few years she'd been coming to the same gym he'd asked her out a few times. Maybe he was what she needed to eradicate the boredom threatening to choke her. Over six feet tall with sandy blond hair, bright blue eyes, and muscles that rivaled Leo's, he definitely held a certain level of appeal. The fact that he was about her age, maybe even a little older, was a bonus. She'd never been all that attracted to blonds, but it couldn't hurt to expand her horizons. Anything would be better than embarrassing herself fawning over her best friend's little brother.

She wiped her towel across her face and walked toward him, plastering on her brightest smile as she went. Her gaze dipped to the embroidered name on his shirt. Steve? Wow. She hadn't even been close.

"Hi, Carla." He beamed, a friendly grin that didn't turn her around, let alone inside out.

She almost gave up and walked away, but she made herself stick it out. Love at first sight, even lust at first sight, was a myth. She'd learned from experience that she had to get to know a man first, before any kind of feelings developed. Except... No. No thinking about *him* any more. "Hi, Steve. How have you been?"

"Great." His smile widened until she wondered if his face would split. "You look terrific. I'm glad to see you keeping up your workouts after so long."

"Thanks." Her inner seductress — where had she been last night when she'd had Leo alone in the laundry room? — urged her to touch his arm, but she couldn't bring herself to do it. She bit back a rough sigh. Even with men who were obviously interested, she couldn't manage to flirt. Why hadn't she paid more attention to the popular girls in high school? "You look good, too."

Heat flashed across his gaze before the comfortable, friendly veneer slipped back into place. "Um, thanks."

She nearly cheered. Maybe she could entice a man after all. *You've got it, girl. Now run with it before you lose your nerve.* "Are you free for coffee sometime?"

Confusion passed across his features, his brow knitting into a frown and the smile slipping. He opened and closed his mouth a few times, looking like he wanted to say something but couldn't come up with the right words.

She crossed her fingers behind her back. Was he going to turn her down? Maybe in the few months since he'd last asked her out, he'd started seeing someone else. He was probably trying to find a gentle way to turn her down. But just as she was about to tell him to forget the whole thing, and find another gym so she didn't have to die of embarrassment every time she saw him, he spoke.

"Yeah. Yeah, that would be great." He laughed, shook his head. "Are you sure, though? Do you mean like a date?"

She let out the breath she hadn't realized she'd been holding. Okay, so maybe his hesitation was for a different reason. "Something like that."

"Well then, yeah. Definitely. That sounds terrific." His smile faltered a little, a nervous expression taking its place. "Are you free this evening, by any chance?"

Talk about cutting to the chase. She nearly shook her head. Had she met the one person more desperate than herself? At least her current misery would be in good company. "That sounds good. It's my day off, so I'm free."

That cute, but not gut-clenching sexy, smile was back in full force. "Excellent. Why don't you meet me back here at seven? There's a great little coffee shop right down the street. We can walk."

His offer to meet her at the gym took a little of the pressure off her. She lived just a few blocks away, so it gave her an out if the date didn't go as planned.

"Sounds great. I'll see you a little later."

She smiled and walked toward the locker room, the whole time her body telling her she'd made a big mistake.

He isn't Leo.

Yeah, that's kinda the point.

Maybe Steve would be able to help her get Leo off her mind before she did something stupid like act on her crazy impulses and embarrassed them both.

* * * * *

"So, tell me about yourself, Carla. Have you ever been married?"

She blinked at Steve across the bright red and yellow mosaic-topped table in the artsy little coffee shop he'd chosen for their date. Had he really just opened with *that* question? What age did a person have to hit before questions like that came into play? A couple more years and her dates would be asking her what her glasses prescription was and if she'd ever had hip replacement surgery. "No. Never. You?"

She tapped her fingernail against her bright yellow coffee mug, nearly as big as a soup bowl. When she'd ordered plain, unflavored coffee with no sugar, the waitress had practically sneered at her. Not a great start to the date, but she still had hopes that they might have *something* in common.

A sheepish grin spread over his mouth. He took a sip of his mocha-java-something and set the mug down before he answered. "Yeah. I got divorced three years ago. We were together for thirteen years, but we'd drifted apart a while before the divorce. We stayed together for the kids, mostly. But when Amy started her freshman year of high school, I just didn't see the point anymore."

Kids? He had kids? And one of them was old enough to be in high school? She swallowed hard and tried to untwist the knot in her stomach. He couldn't be more than three or four years older than her. What a depressing thought. "Wow. You have a daughter in high school?"

He nodded. "She's a senior now. And my son, Matt, is in his second year of college."

Her heart dropped to her toes. *There is no way you have a future with this guy, as adorable as he might be.* He was just about done raising his family, and she hadn't even started yet with hers. What were the odds he'd want to start over again? Pretty much zero. And that left her at square one. *Again.* How was a woman her age supposed to fish for a husband when all the good ones were taken, or finished being taken and ready to have some fun?

Why did that sound so terribly familiar?

Oh yeah. Leo. Most of the men her age she'd met weren't looking for relationships. At least not the married-with-children kind she wanted. A lot of them had already gone that route, or had decided long ago that it didn't interest them. Unfortunately, the younger ones like Leo weren't looking either. So where did that leave her in the grand scheme of things?

Alone. No husband. Hardly any dates. And Leo was ruining the only date she'd had in too long to remember. She might as well pack up and leave now.

And when had she abandoned her search for a hot, illicit fling and gone back to her never ending search for the perfect husband?

No long-term thinking tonight. Bring the focus back to what's important. Sex. Satisfaction. The ability to walk away in the morning, and not feel guilty about it later.

"Are you okay, Carla? You're starting to look a little green."

She blinked and swung her gaze toward Steve. Green, huh? Probably not the best way to entice him into coming back to her apartment after coffee. "Oh. I'm sorry. It's been a long couple of days."

He smiled in understanding, but anxiety tinged his expression. "Does the fact that I have children bother you?"

She opened her mouth to explain the problem, but then thought better of it and snapped her mouth shut. If she told him, he'd think she was crazy. Totally nuts. She nearly laughed at the thought. Maybe she was. It would certainly explain her current pattern of erratic behavior.

The whole situation brought back memories of high school, of trying desperately to find a boyfriend. The more she searched, the less available everyone seemed. Maybe now she needed to relax and let things happen. Who knew? Steve might be just what she was looking for.

After a pot of coffee and a whole lot of awkward conversation, she realized the truth. He wasn't. Not even close. A very pleasant, but completely spark-free hour later she and Steve walked out of the coffee shop. He walked her to her car, bent down and placed a soft, but also spark-free, kiss on her lips.

When he pulled back, a small smile on his face, she sighed. He was so cute, in a big, muscular puppy dog sort of way. Why couldn't she feel passion for someone like him? He had a great body, and she'd be willing to bet he knew how to use it. But there was no chemistry between them. She really enjoyed talking to him, but it wouldn't go any further than that. He knew it as well as she did. She saw the truth in his eyes. She reached up and patted his cheek.

"Thanks for a really nice evening, Steve."

He smiled, brushed his hand over her arm. "I'm sorry it didn't go better."

"Don't be. It was fine."

"Yeah, but I think we were both hoping for more than what we felt."

It figured that the one with-it, appropriate aged, decent-job-holding guy she'd met in recent history met didn't inspire lustful fantasies in the least. Where was the fairness in that? She'd spent almost fifteen years on the search-for-a-husband merry-go-round. Didn't she deserve a break?

"It's okay. I really did have a great time. You're going to make some woman very happy one of these days."

"Tell that to my ex-wife." He laughed. "Yeah, and you'll find who you're looking for. Thanks for going out with me, Carla. I just wish it had gone a little differently, but I hope we can still be friends."

"It was my pleasure." Perhaps pleasure wasn't the right word, seeing as she wouldn't be getting any that night.

"Maybe we can do it again sometime. As friends. I really enjoyed talking to you."

Why did she hear that so often? If she were less friendly, would men want her more? Is that how all those bitchy women got the best guys? "That would be nice."

Steve stood on the sidewalk as she got into her car, started the engine, and drove away down the quiet, night-darkened street. She watched him through her rearview mirror, the whole time wishing something could have come out of that date. *Anything.* He was cute, sexy even, smart, funny, and she really liked talking to him. But she'd embarked on finding the perfect fling, and she wouldn't settle for anything less than everything. She needed lightning. With Steve, there hadn't even been a spark.

She sighed. "Looks like it's back to the beginning."

And why did she want that beginning to be with Leo?

Because she was nuts. Desperately in need of medication. It would pass. It had to. Leo wasn't interested, and there was no way she was setting herself up for rejection with someone like him. It just wasn't worth it.

She ran through her mental list of places to meet eligible men. Church—no. Wouldn't work for a fling. The library—it held definite possibilities. The grocery store? Yeah. That might be her best bet. Plus she'd probably be spending a lot more time there in the coming weeks. With the way her life was going, she was going to need a lot more ice cream.

* * * * *

Leo sat at the bar, slumped on the uncomfortable padded stool, the beer he'd been nursing for hours cupped between his palms. He lifted the bottle to his lips and took a swig, grimacing as the warm liquid slid down his throat and settled like a rock in the pit of his stomach. With a groan, he set the bottle back on the bar.

"What's the matter with you tonight? You aren't acting like your usual self." Cameron settled in on the stool next to Leo and rested his elbows on the bar. He signaled for the bartender and ordered another beer. Cameron's third, maybe fourth for the evening. "There are hundreds of single women in here, and you and Miranda just split a couple weeks ago. I know you've been dating again. Why not tonight? What are you waiting for?"

Carla. "I just need a break from dating. That's all."

"Don't tell me you miss Miranda that much." The bartender slid the open beer bottle in front of Cameron and he took a long pull. "The woman's a flake. Frankly,

I'm surprised you saw her for more than one date, let alone wasting a month of your life with her."

Leo let out a breath filled with pent-up frustration. Miranda. Yeah, Cameron was right. She *was* a flake. But he hadn't dated her for her intelligence. She'd been fun for a while. Just another woman he'd dated to try to get Carla off his mind. "She had a very talented tongue."

Cameron barked a laugh. "Yeah, I knew there had to be some reason. She's kinda lacking in the gray matter department."

"She's a sweet girl." If you like the overblown, porn star look-alike type.

"Oh, really? With the way she constantly crawled all over you, I figured the two of you didn't get in much talking."

He had to laugh at that one. Cameron knew him so well. When they weren't in the bedroom, Miranda had bored him to death. She was too complacent, to willing to bend to whatever he wanted without the least bit of dissention. *Not* the kind of woman who would keep him interested in the long run. "No, talking wasn't one of her strong points. We made better use of our time."

Not that they'd spent much time together, really. In the last week or two of the short time they dated, he'd made excuses to avoid her. She'd been a nice distraction, as they all had, but none of them lasted long enough to erase Carla from his mind. And none of them managed to worm their way into his heart like Carla had so long ago. She was the real deal. The only one who mattered. And it sucked that she seemed to not care. He lifted his bottle to his mouth and drained the last of the liquid.

"Hey, Cam?"

Cameron raised an eyebrow before his gaze shifted to a cute brunette who smiled as she walked by. "Yeah?"

"What's up with you and Carla?"

His gaze snapped back to Leo's, a frown creasing his brow. "Carla? Your sister's friend? The one who cuts my hair?"

"Yeah."

"Why? Did she mention me?"

Leo nodded. Cameron's expression softened and he smiled. "Cool. She's hot."

And you are so not her type. "Sure. You have a thing for her?"

"A thing?" Cameron shuddered. "I don't do anything that remotely resembles serious. You should know that. She's cute. Great body. I'd do her."

And then Leo would have to strangle the man he'd come to consider his closest friend. "She's not like that."

"And how would you know?"

"I've known her my whole life, and she lives right down the hall from me. I'd know if she was bringing men home at all hours of the night." From what he'd seen, she hadn't brought anyone at all home since he'd been living near her. And he'd kept watch. "Trust me. She isn't that kind of woman."

A smile spread over Cameron's face and he burst out laughing. When he finally got control of himself, he smacked Leo on the shoulder. "I don't have a thing for her, buddy, but I think you do."

Was he that obvious? "Nah. She's just a friend. I watch out for her."

"More like you fantasize about her in your bed. Come on, Leo. You've never held out on me before. Why are you suddenly keeping secrets? Spill already."

Leo shook his head. Cameron was right, Leo usually had no problems telling him everything. But for some reason, he held back. This was different. Carla was different. She deserved better than to be the subject of barroom gossip.

"Like I said. She's just a friend." And hopefully more. Very soon.

"Yeah, whatever." Cameron picked up his beer and took another long swig. He set the bottle down with a loud thump and wiped the back of his hand across his lips. "Either you're lying to me, or you're lying to yourself. Either way I don't like it."

Leo glanced around the crowded bar before returning his gaze to Cameron. The hurt in his friend's eyes took him by surprise. "Okay, maybe I do have a thing for Carla. Just a little one. It'll pass."

Cameron smiled. "You don't believe that."

No, he didn't. But it was too early to say anything about what he planned to do. He refused to be embarrassed if things didn't go as he hoped. He just shrugged and let Cameron form his own conclusions.

"Wouldn't it be awkward, getting involved with your sister's friend?" Cameron asked. "I mean, what would happen when it ended? Wouldn't that make things uncomfortable?"

"What if it didn't end?" The words were out of Leo's mouth before he could stop them. He closed his eyes and pinched the bridge of his nose. *Stupid. Really, really damned stupid. Why don't you just give everything away while you're at it, idiot?*

When he opened his eyes, Cameron gaped at him. "What do you mean by that? Are you thinking of settling down? Getting serious? You can't be. I've known you for three years and I've never seen you even remotely serious about anyone."

"Yeah, well, things change sometimes."

"I'll say. This is a complete one-eighty. Are you sure about it?"

Leo shook his head. "At this point I'm not sure about anything. I'm just going to let things flow and see what happens. Maybe she's interested too, and maybe she's not. Only time will tell."

She *was* interested. But would she act on it? If he had anything to say about it, she would.

The brunette who'd smiled at them earlier stepped up to Cameron and ran her hand down his arm. "Wanna dance, handsome?"

"Hey, Tracy. How have you been?"

"Lonely. Care to help me with that?"

Cameron grinned and took her hand in his. "Sure. You got a friend for my buddy? He's pining over someone that's never even gonna look at him twice. Needs something to get his mind off her for a while."

Tracy smiled at Leo, gave him an appraising glance. "I think I can work something out. Michelle and Kelly are here somewhere."

She grabbed Leo's hand and pulled him out of his seat. "Come with me. We'll find you someone to get your mind off more serious matters."

Leo tugged his hand out of her grasp and shook his head. Michelle didn't appeal to him in the least, and Kelly…their one date had proven their incompatibility. "No, thanks. I've got an early morning tomorrow. I think I'm just going to head home."

He took out his wallet and slapped a couple of bills on the bar. "I'll see you at work in the morning, Cam."

Cameron caught up with him before he reached the door. "Are you sure? You're passing up something really good here. Michelle's got a talented tongue, too, along with other parts. She can tie a cherry stem in a knot with her tongue. And that tongue ring… Let me just say that it's friggin' incredible."

Leo laughed, despite the growing sense of unease in his stomach. "As tempting as that sounds, I meant what I said earlier. I need to take a break from dating for a little while. It's just left me unsettled lately. I'll see you tomorrow."

He walked out of the bar, leaving Cameron gaping at him as he stepped out the door. As interesting as Michelle sounded, he could think of a thousand things he'd rather do with his time. No matter what happened with Carla, he had a feeling his days of playing the field were over. He'd grown tired of the dates, tired of the games and one-night stands and waking up alone. Tired of the empty ache of loneliness that had settled in his gut.

He wanted more out of life. Not necessarily a lifetime commitment, not this soon, but something long-term and lasting. A chance to develop familiarity, routine with one woman. Maybe even fall in love. Whatever happened, he was certain of one thing. He wanted meaning in his life. And he'd no longer settle for anything less.

By the time he reached his apartment building, his new resolve had cemented in his head. It was well past time to grow up and stop playing games. First he'd see what happened with Carla, see if there was a chance of anything real developing between them. If what happened didn't turn into something lasting, at least he'd finally be able to put her out of his mind and move on with his life. After years of waiting, pining, trying and not succeeding to get her attention, he was ready to start putting the past aside, one way or another.

But what if she chose Cameron over him?

He fumed at the thought, his gut clenching. If that happened, he'd find himself needing to get some new friends. As willing as he was to ignore his feelings for Carla if what he planned didn't work out, he wouldn't be able to stand by and watch Cameron parade her around at all their usual hangouts. He'd like to think Cameron wouldn't do that to him, but it wouldn't be the first time a man had betrayed a friend for a beautiful woman.

He walked up the stairs and through the doorway that led to his floor. His sour mood brightened when he saw the woman walking up ahead of him. Carla. She looked great, even in something as casual as jeans. So many of the women he dated were obsessed with their weight, losing the ten pounds they thought they had to lose when in reality they had the figures of prepubescent boys. Carla wasn't like that. She'd eaten with his family enough over the years for him to learn that weight, and watching her calorie intake, weren't the most important things in her life. She wasn't overweight, but she wasn't skinny, either. Her curves were perfect. Mouthwatering. The stuff his dreams were made of.

And if he played his cards right, soon they'd be his. He smiled and walked toward her.

* * * * *

Carla unlocked her apartment and pushed the door open. The evening hadn't gone as planned, but it could have gone worse. At least they hadn't ended the evening with her wanting to dump her coffee over his head. Or with her yawning the entire time and nearly falling asleep in her meal like she had with her few most recent dates. Her mother would have told her she was getting closer to finding her Mr. Right. Carla nearly laughed at the absurdity of it all. If the only thing that distinguished Mr. Right from the rest of the men on the planet were the ability to not bore her into a coma, she'd be perfectly happy spending the rest of her life single. It just wasn't worth the trouble.

"Hey, sexy."

She spun to find Leo standing a few feet behind her, a half-smile on his face and his eyes sparkling with amusement. The top two buttons of his white dress shirt were undone and his dark red and black tie hung loose around his neck. She swallowed hard. *Wow.* What right did he have to look so darned good when she probably looked like she'd been dragged through the mud?

"Ha, ha. Very funny." She waited for him to deny that his words were a joke, hoping against hope that he would tell her he really meant it, but of course he didn't. He laughed.

"How's it going, Carla?"

She tried to shrug off the disappointment, but failed miserably. It ate at her insides and threatened to take over her thoughts. "Fine. Hot date again tonight?"

"Not me. What about you? You look great."

In jeans and a black T-shirt? She looked like she was going grocery shopping, which was what she should be doing, if she planned to meet men. "If you say so. I did have a date tonight."

"Oh yeah?" His eyes darkened and his smile fell flat. "How'd it go?"

Was that disappointment that flashed across his gaze? Nah. Couldn't be. Still, she grinned on the inside with the thought that her having a date could get to him. "Great."

His smile was back, knowing, taunting, and he took a couple of steps toward her. "I'm sure it was terrific. And that's why you're home so early."

"I'm not in my twenties, Leo. Not every date has to end in the bedroom." Although it might not hurt for one or two of them to end that way. Hell, at this point she'd be happy with an earth-shattering kiss in the hallway. *Interested in helping me with that, Leo?*

"I didn't mean it like that." He stepped even closer, stopping a few inches from her and sending her pulse skyrocketing. "You don't look happy. That's all I meant. I hope I didn't insult you."

She frowned, though her face flamed. "I'm happy. Very happy." *Especially with you so close, driving me crazy with your warmth and your scent.*

"Yeah. Right." He shook his head, leaned in to her a fraction of an inch. His nose brushed her hair and he drew a deep breath. "Have I mentioned that I love your shampoo?"

"No. I don't think you have." She took a step away from him, into her apartment. *Chicken.* "I…um…I should go to bed now."

"This early?" His eyes darkened and his throat worked as he swallowed. "Alone?"

"Of course alone. Do you see anyone else around here?"

"Nope. Just you and me." Humor danced in his eyes, along with something else. Something darker. Desire? No. Couldn't be anything like that. He was just teasing her, as he'd been doing for years.

So why didn't he back away? Why did he come closer the further away she got? Why did it seem like he was flirting with her? Seducing her, even?

Because her depraved mind was making the whole thing up. He wasn't really interested. He was just playing with her, as he had on so many other occasions over the years. This was no different, at least not on his part. She'd gone so long without sex her fantasies had started taking over reality. She needed to get over her silly and sudden infatuation before she did something they'd both regret.

"Do you need something, Leo?"

A single dark brow rose and a short laugh escaped his throat. "That's a loaded question if I ever heard one."

Her face flamed even hotter and her stomach clenched. *Geez, Carla. Can you act like any more of a wanton idiot?* "Sorry. I…ah, didn't mean it like that."

"It wouldn't bother me if you did."

She froze. She had to have heard him wrong, because there was no way in hell he would be hitting on her. Ever. She'd seen the women he dated. Skinny, young little waifs barely out of college. Most of them cute blondes who would look right at home in a cheerleader uniform. None of them had wrinkles around their eyes, and she'd be willing to bet that they hadn't ever looked into the mirror to find gray hair. He had no reason to hit on someone so totally wrong for him when all he had to do was go inside his apartment and call one of his bimbos to come over and keep him company.

She'd be a fool to even get her hopes up. Her mind warned her to retreat, but her body edged closer. So close his breath brushed her cheek. The scent of beer reached her nose. *Ah.* That explained his behavior. He hadn't gone crazy. He'd been drinking.

"You didn't drive home, did you?"

He frowned down at her. "Why do you ask?"

"You were out at a bar tonight, huh?"

He shook his head, a mixture of amusement and irritation clouding his gaze. "I had one beer. Hardly enough to impair my driving abilities."

"Just one?"

He nodded, his gaze darkening as the irritation overpowered the amusement. "Yes, Carla. Just one. I might be young, but I'm not stupid."

And he wasn't drunk either. Not from one beer. It might be enough to do her in, but for someone of his size, especially a guy who was a regular part of the bar scene, it wouldn't even make a dent in his sobriety.

Then why did it feel like he was still hitting on her? What reason could he possibly have for getting so close? She shook her head and backed into her apartment. "Well, I'm glad to hear that you were being sensible. It was nice talking to you. I really do have to get to bed now."

He didn't move, and his dark, smoldering expression didn't lighten. "I'm sorry your date didn't go well tonight, Carla. You obviously deserve someone better."

Someone like you? Nah. She smiled. "Thanks. That means a lot. Goodnight, Leo. I'll talk to you sometime later."

She stepped inside her apartment and closed the door, leaning against the cool wood. With her body on fire just from talking to him, she had a feeling it was going to be another in a long string of sleepless nights.

Chapter Three

❧

"I swear, if this day gets any worse, I'm going to jump off my balcony," Carla muttered to herself as she walked down the hall to her apartment. Her sexy, very expensive, *foot-torturing* shoes clacked obscenely on the portions of wood floor with every step, driving her out of her mind.

She paused, kicked them off, and considered chucking them out the window at the end of the hall. In the end, sanity prevailed and she tucked them into her black shoulder bag. Agonizing or not, she couldn't justify tossing them out when they'd cost almost as much as she normally paid for groceries in a month. A stupid move, but being a woman entitled her to one or two impulse buys a year.

Okay, a week.

But they were *shoes*. She'd do her Aunt Vivian, the Imelda Marcos of southern New England, proud.

If she kept going this way, she'd have to move into a bigger apartment just to store her footwear. At the price she paid for the evil pumps, she should just buy a curio cabinet and display the stupid things as modern art. At least then they'd get some use, something besides becoming dust bunny condos at the bottom of her closet. The throbbing in her temples intensified at the thought.

On top of the foot ache, she also had a killer headache. Apparently her body didn't like cucumber and sprout sandwiches, because as soon as she'd returned to the salon after her lunch break, her head had launched a rebellion. As much as she'd love to eat pizza or steak subs every day, she had to make an offering to the goddess of weight management once in a while or pay the price. Visions of Aunt Edna and the tents she passed off as dresses danced in Carla's mind, taunting her with the family gene pool and its effects on Michaels women over thirty.

Not a pretty thought.

It was only a matter of time. She'd made it to thirty-five relatively unscathed, but it wasn't for lack of effort. Salads and veggie sandwiches had become the norm at lunchtime, and she dragged herself to the gym nearly every morning to sweat off the fattening salad dressing. But the sad truth kept poking in its big, ugly head. When it all came down to it, none of her efforts would matter. As the years ticked by, the dormant fat cells resting in her hips bided their time, waiting for the signal from her DNA. One day she'd wake up and—*wham!*—thunder thighs.

Well, she wouldn't go down without a—

"Oof." She slammed into something hard and warm, and breathing, bringing her mental whining to a screeching halt.

Oh boy. Her neighbors already thought she was nutty enough. They didn't need any more ammunition.

"I'm so sorry. I wasn't watching where…" Her voice trailed off as she looked up at the person she'd almost barreled over in her mental quest to fight the inevitability of heredity.

Leo.

And here she'd thought the day couldn't *possibly* get any worse.

Why was it that she had to run into him at the end of every bad day, the end of every bad date? She couldn't ever bump into him when she was on her way out the door to work, her hair and makeup done and her morning coffee just taking effect. No, it had to be when she looked her worst that she ran right into him. Her face flamed and she backed up a step, not taking into account that wearing those shoes all day had numbed her feet, and lost her balance. She teetered backward for an endless second before she toppled toward the floor. Her stomach bottomed out and she braced herself for the smack of the hardwood against her rump, but it never came.

Instead, strong arms hauled her back onto her feet, pulling her right up against a hard chest. *Leo's chest.* His hand smoothed down her back in what should have been a comforting gesture, but it sucked the breath right out of her like a strong wind.

"Are you okay?" he asked, his breath hot against the side of her neck. His lips brushed her earlobe and a shiver ran the length of her body. Another few minutes like this and she'd melt into a puddle at his feet.

"I'm fine." She wriggled, struggling to pull out of his arms before she lost all powers of rational thought. He would *not* appreciate being attacked when all he'd wanted to do was help. "Would you mind letting me go?"

"Oh, sorry." He laughed and pulled back, giving her body a cursory glance before his gaze settled on her face. His frown made her want to whip her compact out of her bag to see if she had any leftover sprouts stuck between her teeth.

He cupped her cheek in his palm, smoothed his thumb down the side of her face, sending a shiver from her head to her toes before he dropped his hand to his side. "Are you sure you're okay? You look a little flushed."

Flushed? *Major* understatement. If she got any redder steam would come out of her ears. At least she had an excuse this time, one that didn't involve being pressed into a hard male chest. "I have a headache."

"A headache, huh?" His slow, hot smile rocked her right down to her shoeless feet, sending a wave of heat knifing through her belly. "I know the perfect cure for that."

She rolled her eyes. Leave it to a man to ruin the mood. The heat inside her evaporated into an icy chill at his suggestion as she mentally reiterated the mantra she'd learned in high school and almost never forgot. *Men are pigs.* Apparently, even the sexy ones were no exception. "I think I can take care of it myself, thanks. I don't need any of your *cures*."

"Are you sure? My mom's chicken soup is rumored to have mystical healing qualities."

Soup? She closed her eyes against the extreme embarrassment flooding her. She'd done it again, assuming things. Seeing signals that just weren't there. She'd have to learn to stop the foolishness, or steer clear of the man before she made a fool out of herself. "I, ah…"

Apparently, he misread her current state of speechlessness. He held his hands in front of him, palms up, his expression a little bit worried. "I know you need your rest, but trust me on this one. This stuff really works. I have a container in the freezer. I know you're tired from work, but I can heat it up in a couple of minutes. I'll have you back home in a half hour, tops, and you'll feel much better."

Her heart flipped. He was offering to cook for her. How often did a man offer to cook for a woman, and not have some twisted ulterior motive? Granted, he'd only offered to reheat something someone else had made for him, but she'd be an idiot to pass up a once in a lifetime offer like that. She'd been single so long she'd forgotten what it was like to have someone else do things for her. It would be nice for a change to relax and let him do the work. "You don't mind?"

He took her arm and steered her toward his apartment. "Nope. I've had bad days myself, so I understand what you're going through. Hey, I'm always willing to help a friend in need."

A friend in need. A *friend* in need. She really had to stop misreading his *friendly* actions as come-ons, or she would find herself in a heap of trouble. The man had no lustful feelings toward her, and he never would. He probably had a whole list of twenty-somethings ready and willing whenever he called. Hell, she knew he did. She'd seen the endless parade of women going in and out his door.

The little voice inside her head reminded her of his lips brushing her ear, but she quashed that voice before it could protest too loudly. His lips hadn't brushed any part of her body. Her sex-deprived mind had probably made it up. Chalk the whole electrically charged incident up to wishful thinking and going months too long without more than a single date or a single goodnight kiss.

"First dinner," he told her as he let her go to open his apartment door. "And then we'll see what we can do about curing that headache."

Hold on a second. "I thought you said the food *was* the cure?"

He gave her a playful wink that did funny things to her insides. "That's just a rumor. I happen to know of a *much* better solution."

What was his game now? She tried to brush off the shivers running the length of her spine, but the amusement dancing in his eyes made that impossible. Did he find it fun to torture her? "What is it? Aspirin?"

His raised eyebrow and secretive smile was answer enough. *Definitely not aspirin.* Could it be that his interest in her was real, and not just her imagination?

The little voice started to chime in again with its useless opinions. Leo's hand brushed her bare arm and the voice wisely shut up.

* * * * *

Leo stole a sidelong glance across the kitchen as he stuck the plastic container of soup into the microwave. Carla sitting at his kitchen table had to be one of his biggest fantasies.

Or was that sitting *on* the table?

Oh yeah. *Definitely.* Sitting on the table, wearing…well, nothing. Except maybe those spiky-heeled black shoes that had spilled out of her bag when she tossed it onto the counter. He could go for that. Carla on his table, every inch of her fair skin bared to his eyes, her—

He cleared his throat, hoping to bring himself back to reality, or at least a reasonable facsimile. She didn't feel well. This wasn't the time to be hitting on her, even though it was definitely the right place. Any lascivious thoughts would have to be shelved until she felt better. "What do you want to drink? I have beer, red wine, cola, orange juice…"

"Just water is fine, if you don't mind." She gave him a fleeting smile, her gaze laced with fatigue and pain. He felt like a heel for even thinking about getting her naked, but the image held a lot of appeal. Had for too many years to count.

Even ill and stressed, Carla was gorgeous. He had a weakness for redheads, with her being a particular favorite. Hell, she was probably the reason he had a thing for red hair in the first place. She'd been his first crush. His first fantasy. And if he didn't stop the train of thought, he'd end up making a fool out of himself and losing any chance he might have with her. The thought sobered him. Marginally. At least enough that he could focus on moving away from the counter to the sink and filling a glass with water. For Carla. Who had a headache and didn't need to know about the thirty-plus different ways he wanted to take her. And that was before they even made it to the bedroom.

He set the glass in front of her, along with a small bottle of ibuprofen, leaning in close enough to get a good whiff of her shampoo-scented hair. Peaches and vanilla. She'd used the same kind for as long as he could remember, and he couldn't smell it without memories assaulting him—memories of the time when he was eighteen and had accidentally walked in on her in the shower. She'd been twenty-eight at the time, and staying with his family for a few weeks while waiting for her new apartment to be ready. He hadn't been able to look her in the eye for the rest of her stay, and the images of her naked and slick with water had fueled a number of his teenage fantasies. To this day, he still got hard at just the thought.

Even now, when he should be old enough to have control over his body, his groin stirred to life.

Damn. He'd go out of his mind if this kept up any longer. He had to do something to take this thing between them to the next level before he exploded.

At this rate, he figured that would take about an hour.

But not tonight. Tonight she needed someone to take care of her, not someone to take advantage. He'd learned a thing or two growing up in a female-dominated household. His mother and sisters had made sure to teach him to be sensitive to a woman's needs, and how to pamper a woman when she needed it. Tonight he'd take care of Carla. Convincing her to give him a chance could wait until another night.

He pulled a chair close to her and sat down, lifting her leg and settling her foot on his thigh. Without giving her a chance to protest, he ran the heel of his hand up the center of her sole.

"Leo, don't. My feet hurt. I don't need to be tickled right now."

"Tickling is most definitely *not* what I have in mind. I'm just trying to relax you. You're so tense I'm afraid you're going to snap." He smiled at her uncertain expression. "Trust me, Carla. Just sit still. You eat, and I'll help you loosen up."

Though her idea of loosening up would be very different from what he considered.

She squirmed under his touch at first—how she managed to down half the bowl of soup without spilling a drop amazed him—but after a few minutes relaxed back against the chair and closed her eyes.

"This is nice." A soft sigh escaped her lips as his hands moved up her calf. "*Wow.*"

"Nice" didn't even begin to describe what was happening. It took all his willpower not to groan out loud. A few more inches and her toes would brush the zipper of his pants and she'd know, with complete certainty, how she affected him. The feel of her silky skin under his hands sent jolts all the way up his arms, as well as to a few other places. In his wildest fantasies he'd never dreamed he'd have her this close, her legs bared to his touch. Five years ago, he would have been too nervous to know what to do with her. But a lot had changed in recent years.

"Glad I could be of service." If he scooted back just a little, he might be able to get a glimpse up her skirt. "Aren't you going to eat any more?"

"Eat? You've got to be kidding me. I feel so liquid I don't even know if I could hold the spoon."

Exactly the way he wanted her. He lifted her other foot into his lap and went to work, earning a small moan for his efforts, which increased the tightening in his groin to a painful level.

"Where did you learn how to do this?" she asked, catching him by surprise.

"I dated a massage therapist. She showed me a few tricks of the trade."

"Oh, really? Interesting. She taught you well." He caught a hint of jealousy in her reply and laughed to himself. He'd never tell her that Jessica broke up with him because he'd called her Carla in bed.

"Yeah, so I've heard." Nothing wrong with a little jealousy to increase her interest.

Her eyebrows rose, suspicion clouding her eyes. "And have you had many opinions?"

Why did it feel like they were no longer talking about massages? He thought for a second about denying the truth, but didn't see how it would do much good. She lived close enough to know a little about his dating life. And it couldn't hurt to give her another push toward thinking of him as a man rather than a kid. "Yeah, I suppose I have. Enough to know what I'm doing, and to be able to do it well."

"Is that so?"

A corner of his mouth rose in a half-smile. His gaze locked with hers, his hands never leaving her foot. When he spoke, he didn't raise his voice much past a low whisper. "I've *never* had any complaints, Carla. Only praise. And *plenty* of that. Screaming, moaning, back-clawing praise."

She sucked in a ragged gulp of air, moistened her lips with the tip of her pink tongue. "*Oh.*" The single word came out on a sigh.

An electrically charged silence settled over the room, Carla's face flushing and her hands fidgeting in her lap.

Then her gaze dropped to *his* lap, and the obvious erection he couldn't conceal.

Her eyes widened and she dropped her foot, pushing up out of the chair, grabbing her bag, and moving across the room before he even had a chance to blink. "Well, thanks for the soup. And the ibuprofen. I appreciate it. It helped a lot. I have to go, though. Early morning, you know?"

He stood as well, moving toward her until his body came within inches of hers. She gulped, backed up a step, and it took all his willpower not to pull her against him. He pasted on his best friends-only smile, trying to turn things down a notch before he scared her away with his enthusiasm.

"No problem. That's what friends are for, right?" Friends. Ha! Every time he said the word, it nearly killed him. He'd never wanted to be her friend, at least not *only* her friend. If everything worked according to his plan, they'd be so much more than the friends she thought they were now. She was fooling herself, thinking that the only thing between them was friendship. Since the encounter in the laundry room, things between them had changed. There was an electricity that he'd never noticed before, and by her current state of nervousness he knew she felt it, too. Now he just had to figure out what to do to get her to stop denying it.

She stood and stretched her arms over her head, her blouse pulling tight across her breasts and lifting to reveal a delectable inch of smooth, creamy midriff. His mouth went dry at the sight and he leaned in, prepared to finally take what he wanted and kiss her.

"Friends," she repeated softly, an odd smile on her face. "That's the second time you've said that tonight. Do you really consider me a friend?"

Ah, damn. He couldn't kiss her now, not when she acted all sappy and cute. Yes, he considered her a friend, but damn it, it wasn't nearly enough. He needed so much more, but guilt kicked in and reminded him he wasn't going to get it. At least not tonight. "Yeah, I do." Yeah, he had a soft side, but he'd never admit it aloud. Especially not to her.

"That's sweet." An uncertain expression crossed her face, but it was gone before he could interpret it. She stuffed her shoes back into her bag, slipped the bag over her shoulder, and walked toward the door. "Thanks again, Leo. I'll talk to you later."

"Yeah. Later."

When his gaze fell to that cute, curvy butt swaying underneath the flowery skirt, the truth of the matter smacked him in the chest.

He *could* kiss her.

No problem.

Sure, he might feel guilty in the morning, but he was a guy. It was his job to do stupid things he'd regret later—or at least that's what his mother and sisters seemed to believe. It wouldn't be fair to anyone to correct that assumption now, of all times, when the woman of his dreams looked disappointed as she walked away.

He strode to the door just as she started to open it and slapped his palm against it. The door slammed shut with a bang. Carla stopped short and spun around to face him. She let out a startled gasp, which he quickly covered.

With his lips.

Amazing. Absolutely, utterly, incredibly amazing. He'd always known it would be like this—hot and sweet and familiar all rolled into one scorching kiss he didn't want to end. But his fantasies hadn't even come close to reality. She melted against him, her breasts crushed against his chest, his skin greedily sucking in all the heat she radiated. His blood pounded in his ears, making hearing impossible, and his heart threatened to beat right out of his chest.

He put everything he had into the kiss, every emotion he didn't dare utter aloud, every thought and dream he'd ever had about her. Still one small part of him waited for her to push him away, call him a pig for taking advantage of the situation.

She didn't.

Instead, she wrapped her arms around his neck and pulled him closer, thrusting her tongue between his parted lips.

The fine thread holding his control intact snapped. He backed her into the wall, pressing his body into hers. Her hands skimmed down his back, settling above the waistband of his jeans, and she moaned into his mouth. His arousal ratcheted up another notch as the kiss turned into a flash fire burning out of control. He cupped her face in his hands and angled her head to deepen the contact.

Still, she didn't protest. Didn't utter a word when his hands left her face and traveled down her body, cupping her breasts in his palms. His thumbs skimmed over her peaked nipples, but it wasn't enough. He craved more. All of her he could get his hands on. He pushed his hands under the soft fabric of her shirt, struggled to move her bra out of the way until he held her bare breasts against the heated skin of his hands. Even then, when he'd taken liberties he wouldn't have thought to take with her so soon, she made no move to escape. She moaned and threaded her hands through his hair, not allowing him opportunity to break the kiss.

As if that would ever have happened.

Her damp skin scorched his palms, and she smelled sweet. Peaches and vanilla and warm, sexy woman. God, he was so lost.

That thought was enough to break the sensual spell and tumble him back to reality. He'd promised himself to take it slowly with her, and he meant to stick with that, no matter how frustrated he was. For now he'd have to live with hot dreams and cold showers, stolen kisses and brief touches. Just until he could convince her that they belonged together for more than a fling. If he hadn't been certain of that before, he was now. Their electrifying kiss had proven to him that he wanted more from Carla than a quick screw. He wanted everything.

He broke the kiss, almost losing his resolve when she gripped his waist and tried to pull him closer. His hands dropped from her breasts, his fingers working to straighten her bra and shirt as best as he could.

His lips brushed the tip of her nose and he rested his forehead against hers. The rasp of their panting breaths surrounded him, her scent still flooding his senses. He allowed himself a moment to relish in the feel of her so close, so available and willing, before he stepped back and opened the door.

He smiled down at her, her glazed-over expression mirroring the fog in his mind. What he wouldn't give to have her look at him like that, when he was over her in his bed, pounding into the warmth of her body.

But not tonight.

"Goodnight, Carla."

The image of her aroused and mussed from his kiss, hot and ready to join him in his bed, would be what he saw as he fell asleep that night. Assuming he got any sleep, with his level of frustration teetering on the edge of meltdown proportions. But he'd made the right decision. She wasn't one to rush into things, and taking her to bed that night would only chase her away in the end. It would be more gratifying for both of them to wait, though his body was greatly protesting.

"Goodnight?" She blinked a few times before the glazed look subsided. It nearly killed him to see it replaced by embarrassment. She darted her tongue out to wet her lips, her gaze dropping to the floor. "Oh, yeah. Goodnight."

She stepped out the door, wobbling a little on unsteady legs. After she'd made it down the hall to her own apartment, she glanced back at him. "Thanks again for the soup, Leo. Sleep well."

Sleep? Ha! Not bloody likely.

Chapter Four

֍

"Have you even listened to a *word* I've said?"

Carla blinked her bleary eyes open and faced Alice across her kitchen table. "Huh?"

Alice let out an annoyed snort and set her mug of tea down with a dull thud. "I asked you if you were feeling okay. You look a little pale, and you have gigantic bags under your eyes."

Carla's fingers flew to her face, prodding the puffy skin she'd already spied in the mirror first thing that morning. Nope. Hadn't gone down a bit. After a night of zero sleep, thanks to Alice's little brother and his breath-stealing, toe-curling, sensibility-exploding kiss, she should have expected something like this. Her face heated. She jerked her mug off the table and brought it to her lips, splashing her now-lukewarm tea all over herself and the table in the process.

Alice only sighed as she pushed up from her chair and grabbed the dishcloth to mop up Carla's mess. "See what I mean? There's something wrong with you. Maybe you should call a doctor."

Yeah, a shrink, because she'd be out of her mind if she thought Alice would ever accept her sudden infatuation with Leo. Alice, the original overprotective sister, hated every woman Leo had ever brought home. And according to Alice, there had been quite a few. And those were only the ones he'd allowed his family to meet.

Family. They posed another problem. Her parents, ex-hippies who'd had almost named their only child Flower, wouldn't care as long as she was happy. But Leo's parents were a different story. Mrs. Spencer had dreams for her son—dreams of him marrying a nice young woman and settling down to have a family. What would she think if she knew Carla, a woman she'd trusted to baby-sit the younger Spencer children, had nearly attacked her son and ripped his clothes off? Alice, who was nine months younger than Carla, was the oldest of the five Spencer children. Leo was the youngest. That didn't say a lot for Carla's judgment.

But he's twenty-five. Well past the age of being a legal adult and very able to make his own decisions.

She shoved the away the devil inside her head yet again. It didn't matter how old he was, or how capable he was of making his own decisions. They had a history together. One that did *not* usually lead to romantic involvement.

And then there was Alice. She hated to think how Alice would react now, with her pregnancy-riddled hormones in control of her common sense. She shuddered, remembering how Alice had responded when she'd been told that the cook at Manny's Diner couldn't make pancakes and sausages at nine o'clock at night.

That poor little waitress would never be the same.

No, confessing her illicit fantasies to Alice wouldn't be an option. She'd have to pretend that everything was normal, when in reality her world had become a snow globe. Turned upside down and shaken so everything scattered and nothing fell back into the place it had been.

She forced a weak smile and tried to slow the rapid-fire beating of her heart. "I'm fine. I didn't get much sleep last night."

"Hmm. Nikki's giving you too many hours at work again, isn't she?"

Carla let out a relieved sigh, thankful for the change of subject. Though she'd never understand why Alice worried so much about her hours at work. It wasn't like she had anything better to do with her time. Up until recently, her social life had been so lacking she'd been thinking of buying it a plot in the cemetery. At least work kept her mind off the fact that she'd be forty in five years and had yet to find Mr. Right. "Of course not. Work's been great. Fantastic, even."

"Oh yeah, I bet. It's a dream job. Standing on your feet all day, putting your hands in a bunch of strangers' hair. Sounds like an absolute blast."

Carla rolled her eyes. No one, not even her best friend, understood why she'd dropped out of college in her second year and signed up for cosmetology school. When she nodded off in the middle of a history final exam, she took it as a hint to get out before she bored herself into an early grave. The fact that, as an eight-year-old, she'd cut and styled her dolls' hair and dyed it with gelatin powder should have been an early indication of where her life was headed. And working in Scarlet, a high-end salon, she made more money than she would have as the elementary school teacher she'd originally planned to be. She had to support her shopping habit somehow.

"I love my job. I really do. I can't picture myself doing anything else."

Of course, she had pictured herself married with three or four kids by now, but *that* hadn't gone as planned. She considered herself a liberated woman — to a point. She drew the line at raising a family alone, and she refused to settle for a wishy-washy relationship when she could have it all.

Unfortunately, *all* now seemed to involve Leo and his bone-melting kiss. She had to find some way to get him out of her system so she could settle down with a man who had goals and dreams that actually matched hers, instead of worrying about when the next party would be, and what woman he'd take home the following Friday night.

Forget the fact that she wanted to be that woman. Since their encounter in the laundry room, she'd done nothing but think about what it would be like to be with him, even for just one night. In her fantasies he was loving and attentive, and made sure she was always satisfied. Though in real life, she doubted it would be that good. In her experience, real life, real sex, never even came close to what her mind could think up.

"I think Leo is seeing someone new." Alice's words jerked Carla back to the present so hard her teeth knocked together. "He won't tell me who it is, but he's been acting all…mushy for the last couple of days."

Mushy? She'd seen intense, sensual. So hot he scorched her fingertips. But mushy? Not even close. She swallowed hard and took a deep breath. *Drop the subject, Alice. You don't want to go there.* "Maybe he's embarrassed about her, and he doesn't want you to meet her."

And why wouldn't he be embarrassed? He'd apparently lost his mind.

Alice wrinkled her nose as she took another sip of tea. "Or maybe he's really serious about this one, and he doesn't want me to scare her away."

Carla's mouth went dry. He hadn't said anything, had he? He'd better not have. If Leo even thought about mentioning their kiss, she would kill him. Nobody needed to know about it. Ever. *It wasn't serious.* Not even close. "I doubt that's it. You know Leo. He's never serious about anything."

Alice snorted, shook her head. A look of abject disbelief shot across her expression. "Where have you been for the last five years? Leo's changed a lot. Now he's serious about *everything*. Well, except women. That's what makes me wonder about this new one. He's acting different than he has before. Almost like he actually cares for this one."

Her heart skipped a beat. She did *not* need Alice to find out that she was the new woman in Leo's life. And he most certainly didn't care for her, at least not in the way Alice thought. "How can you even be sure there *is* one?"

"Oh, I know, Carla. I *always* know. I just wish he'd pick someone good for him this time. The women he usually dates are so wrong for him it isn't funny. It's like he purposely goes after the ones he knows he'd never have a future with."

Carla gulped. That would explain why he was suddenly pursuing her. "Maybe he just isn't ready to settle down."

"Well, what is he waiting for? 2030? Come on. He's twenty-five. He has a great job and a nice apartment. And he's the sweetest guy I know. He has a lot to offer a woman. The *right* woman."

"But—"

"What are you arguing so much for? Do you know something I don't?" Alice's dark brows knit together in a frown. "Your cheeks are red. Do you have a fever? Are you sick?"

Thank God for pregnancy-induced forgetfulness. Maybe Alice would let the subject of Leo and his mystery woman drop for good this time.

"No. No fever." But she'd been burning up last night. How he'd had that effect on her with just one kiss was a question for modern science to answer.

But, as Alice said, he only went after the wrong women. He didn't want to settle down. She did. She drew another strike against them on her mental chalkboard. He just wanted a quick fling. Which, she had to keep reminding herself, was what she was supposed to be looking for, too.

Wasn't it?

Alice's lips curled into a knowing smile. "Okay, Carla. Spill."

Carla gestured to her shirt. "I already did."

"Ha, ha. I'm serious. Who is the guy that has you in such knots?"

Oh yeah, like I'm ever going to confess that one to you. She valued her life enough to keep her mouth shut on that particular subject. "Give me a break. There is no guy."

A knock sounded on the door, saving Carla from answering any further questions. Their lunch had arrived. That would buy her at least ten minutes to come up with a good story while Alice shoveled down the food. Lying to her best friend left guilt gnawing in the pit of her stomach, but she couldn't help it. This was one of those rare times that she had to think about the future of their friendship.

Or the *lack* of a future if Alice ever discovered Carla's secret fantasies.

She ran to the door and swung it open. She might just have to hug the delivery person from the corner deli for this one.

Or not.

She had a delivery all right, but it wasn't their lunch—not unless the deli had started giving away huge bouquets of flowers with every order.

"I've got a delivery for Carla Michaels," the flowers said. She heard a muffled sneeze, and then a teenager with straggly blond hair poked his head around the vast array of orange and pink petals. "Jeez. Someone must really care about you to send such a big basket." His eyes widened as he took in the sight of her in her old T-shirt and sweats, her hair pulled back in a messy ponytail. "Did you just get out of the hospital or something?"

What ever happened to respecting one's elders? She narrowed her eyes, resisting the urge to smack the kid upside the head. "Very funny."

"Are you going to take these, or what?" He started to hand her the flowers when she heard footsteps coming up behind her.

Alice.

Shit.

No, there's no man in my life. I just like to send myself flowers once in a while. It's good for the ego, you know, and they just make the house smell so pretty. Yeah, right. "Hold that thought," she told him before shutting the door in the poor guy's face.

A second later Alice rounded the corner into the entryway. "What was that all about? Where's our food?"

"Not here yet." Carla blinked, trying her best not to look guilty.

Alice raised her eyebrows. "Not here yet?" she repeated, her tone laced with suspicion. "Oh, really. Then who was just at the door?"

She wracked her brain for a clever excuse, but came up empty. Fine time for her mind to take a vacation. "Wrong number."

Gee, with that quick-thinking wit, it's a wonder you don't have men beating the door down to get to you.

"I mean, wrong apartment. One of those door-to-door salesmen, you know? Looking for Mrs. Phelps on the first floor."

Another knock sounded, and Carla's pulse kicked up another notch or two...or ten. *Get it together, Carla. Don't you think you're overreacting just a bit? You could always tell her the flowers are for your birthday.*

That might have worked, if she hadn't celebrated her birthday two months ago.

"Are you going to answer that?" Alice asked.

"Yeah. Sure." She had to force her hand to wrap around the doorknob and turn. When she pulled the door open, she let out a relieved breath to see a woman next to the guy with the flowers, holding a brown paper sack. Maybe Alice wouldn't notice the flowers in a rush to get to the chicken salad and olive sandwich she'd ordered.

Fat chance.

Alice not only noticed the flowers, but she hurried forward to grab them out of the kid's hands. How she managed to carry them with her belly looking like she'd swallowed a basketball, Carla would never know. "I'll take these into the other room, Carla. You have the perfect place for them, right on top of that little end table you found at the antique store last week. Then I'll set the kitchen table while you pay for the food. Oh, and don't forget to tip the kid extra. These things are heavy. I don't know how he managed to get them up the stairs without falling over."

If only he'd tripped and ruined the bouquet. That would have been the perfect solution.

Alice headed down the hall before Carla could protest. She dug in her purse, finally snagging a couple of bills from her wallet. Praying the little white card she'd spied among the blooms didn't say anything too embarrassing—or name any names—she handed the kid a five and the woman a twenty. "Keep the change," she said to the woman as she slammed the door shut, not even caring that she'd just given her a ten dollar tip. Some things in life were more important than money. Like her friendship with Alice. And her sanity.

She raced back to the kitchen to find Alice standing at the table, the card in her hand. Carla groaned. She might as well start planning her funeral.

"'I can't sleep without seeing you in my dreams.' Huh. He didn't even bother to sign his name," Alice said, her expression a good mix of irritation and curiosity. "You're not seeing anyone, huh? Who sent these, your imaginary friend?"

"Uh…"

Alice shook her head, the hurt in her eyes turning to excitement. "Okay, okay. Don't tell me his name. If he has you this worked up, he must be pretty important to you. I don't know who's being more secretive right now, you or Leo. I'll forgive you, as long as you tell me *everything*. Sit down, Carla. I want details."

Carla sunk into her chair and covered her face with her hands. This was going to be a very long meal.

* * * * *

Leo spent the first few hours of his Saturday morning going over the new batch of web graphics he'd been working on. Or at least he would have, if he hadn't seen Carla's face every time he glanced at the computer screen.

Jesus.

He shouldn't have kissed her. Or maybe he shouldn't have stopped. Now he couldn't stop thinking about how she'd looked when he'd pulled away. All soft eyes and swollen lips and red cheeks—exactly how he imagined she'd look after a night of making love.

Even the thought of making love to Carla had him rock-hard. He groaned and leaned back against the couch, his work forgotten for the moment. If he didn't get her into bed soon…well, it wouldn't be a pretty sight.

Did she get the flowers he'd sent? Did she like them? With any luck, she hadn't thrown them out the window. He hadn't acted respectable the other night, and he hadn't heard from her since. Worry knotted his stomach. Had he screwed everything up? Even if he had, the bouquet should make up for at least some of his asinine, hormonal behavior. Women liked things like flowers, didn't they? He didn't have a lot of experience in the courting department. He'd always made it a point *not* to shower the women he dated with affection. He hadn't wanted any attachments. Even now, the thought of courting Carla had him squirming in his seat. But he *wanted* to do it this time. It would just take some getting used to. And he planned to go all-out with this one.

He'd gone down to the florist and picked the flowers out himself, instead of going online and ordering a dozen red roses like he did for his mother and sisters on their birthdays. With Carla, everything was different. She deserved bright, exotic flowers — ones she'd never forget. He remembered hearing her talking to Alice one time when they were in college and he'd been about eleven or twelve. She'd said she wanted a man to woo her, to treat her like a lady. He hadn't understood what she'd meant at the time, but he hadn't forgotten her words. Now he understood, and her words had helped him form a plan of action. A slow smile spread over his face. When he finished *wooing* her, she wouldn't know what hit her.

He'd been flirting with her for months, and she'd always brushed it off. Acted like it was some big joke, like he couldn't possibly be serious. Like he was some little kid. She hadn't seemed to notice that he'd grown up.

But she would. He'd make sure of it.

A knock on his apartment door pulled him from his thoughts. His heart rose into his throat. Carla? Had she come to thank him for the flowers? Maybe by repeating the kiss they'd shared the other night? He rushed to the door and pulled it open. But it wasn't Carla standing on the other side.

Alice burst through his front door. Well, waddled in considering her current size. The glare on her face and the set of her shoulders made up for what she lacked in speed.

"Hey, Al. What's up?" He asked the question, though he had a sinking suspicion she wasn't there to talk baby names. "What can I do for you?"

"What can you do for *me*?" She put her hands on her hips and shook her head. "How about you start by telling me what the hell is going on with you?"

He gulped. "I have no idea what you're talking about."

"Oh, really?" Her eyes flashed fire. "I think you know exactly what I'm talking about. You've got some serious explaining to do, little brother."

Chapter Five

ജ

Shit.

He took a deep breath, racking his brain for something he may have done wrong in the past few weeks, other than hitting on Alice's best friend. There had to be something he'd done to make her angry. He swore to himself when he couldn't think of a single thing. *Damn it.* She had to be talking about Carla. "Nice to see you, too, Alice."

She made a little sound of disgust that conveyed "stupid male" better than any words could have. "Don't play dumb with me, Leo Mark Spencer. Explain yourself before I have to get violent."

He held back a laugh as he looked her over. At five foot even and a hundred and fifteen pounds hugely pregnant, Alice's threat didn't exactly inspire fear. But she could make a lot of trouble for him with Carla, so he decided to play along. "Can you elaborate a little more? I've done so many stupid things in my life I can't pinpoint which one you're calling me on."

"Oh *really*? Yes, I'll be the first to agree you've done more than your share of asinine things, but this has to top the list." Alice tapped her foot on the floor and glared at him. "What do you think you're doing seeing Carla?"

"She's my neighbor. Of course I'm bound to see her-"

"Don't even go there." Alice stomped past him into the living room, smacking him on the shoulder on the way by. "I don't want to hear any excuses. I saw the card you sent with those flowers. Excellent choice on the bouquet, by the way. Remember those for when this little guy is born." She patted her stomach and smiled before fixing him with another angry stare. "What do you think Mom and Dad are going to say about this?"

Anger rose in him at her words. Pregnant or not, she had no right to come in and talk to him like he was some little kid who couldn't make up his mind. He didn't need her permission, or their parents', to date whoever he wanted. "Why the hell should what Mom and Dad think even be an issue here? What I do in my personal time is my business. No one else's. Not even yours, in case you've forgotten."

"She's ten years older than you."

"So what? Age has nothing to do with how I feel about her. How I've always felt about her." Too late he realized his words. His breath left his lungs in a whoosh of air that nearly choked him.

"I just want to know one thing. Please tell me you're serious about this, that it isn't some fling. If you just want her for a couple of nights, you need to back off right now."

"It's..." His voice trailed off as he watched Alice's expression go from furious, to annoyed, and on to pleading. What did she want him to say? Did she *want* him to want something serious with Carla? It looked that way.

Women. Sometimes they could be way too complicated. If they just said what they felt instead of all the hints and suggestions they dropped endlessly, the world would be a much more peaceful place. At least there wouldn't be so many confused men running around, wondering what they did wrong. Did they think men were mind readers? "Um…"

"*Um?* Is that all you have to say for yourself? You've been sleeping with my best friend—a fact I don't appreciate being kept from me, thank you very much—for God knows how long, and all you have to say for yourself is *um*? Don't you think—?"

"I'm not sleeping with her," he interrupted quietly.

Alice snapped her mouth shut and blinked up at him. It took a full, uncomfortable minute before she spoke again, her tone hesitant. "What do you mean you're not sleeping with her?"

"Just what I said. I have never had sex with Carla."

Alice looked so surprised that he had to hold back another laugh.

"Didn't she tell you?" *Please say she told you and I didn't just make a huge, complete fool out of myself for nothing.*

"No. I asked her and asked her, but she wouldn't tell me anything. Right up until the flowers were delivered, she tried to pretend she wasn't involved with anyone." The beginnings of a sly smile played on Alice's mouth, a look that meant big trouble. "She doesn't know that I know it's you who sent the flowers."

Interesting. "If she didn't tell you, then how did you know I sent them?" If she didn't warn Carla away from him, maybe she wasn't as upset as he had first thought. He flopped down on the couch and propped his feet up on the coffee table, patting the cushion next to him. "Sit down, Alice, before your ankles swell."

She snorted in a very unladylike manner as she waddled over and slowly lowered herself to the couch.

"Anyone who knows you well would know you wrote out that card. Your handwriting. It's very…distinct."

Horrendous described it better. Growing up, his parents had always joked that he should become a doctor. He already had the handwriting for it. "So, what *did* she tell you?"

Alice sighed and leaned back against the couch, her hand massaging her huge middle. "She said she's seeing someone, but that it's too new to blab about it yet."

For some reason, Alice's words sent a pang of disappointment through him. "Is that *all*?"

"Well… She might have said a few more things." Humor danced across Alice's expression. He let out a rough sigh. He'd never hear the end of this.

"Tell me."

Her smile was nothing short of devilish. "How much are you going to pay me?"

He barked a laugh. She hadn't fooled him with that game in too many years to count, and she knew it. "Never mind. I think I'll just go ask her myself."

Her eyes widened. "No. Don't do that."

"Why not?"

"I don't want her to know that I know. It would make things too awkward, especially when you break up."

Oh, for God's sake. She'd already doomed the relationship, and they'd barely gotten it started. "Ali, I told you that Carla and I are *not* seeing each other." Yet. "There can't be a breakup if there isn't a relationship first." And if he had anything to say about it, there wouldn't be a breakup at all once he'd talked her into the relationship.

Alice plucked a design magazine from the pile on the end table next to the couch and leafed through it, shaking her head. "Okay. Fine. If you say so. Just answer me one question, Leo."

"Fine. One."

"Do you still have a huge crush on her?"

Crush? It had gone past a crush and into far more serious territory in the past couple of years. *Way past.* He opened his mouth to reply, but no sound came out.

Alice just smiled. "I thought so. Just don't do anything stupid, okay? She's my best friend and I don't want to lose her because you don't know how to keep your hands to yourself. I know how you are, Leo. I know how you treat women and I have to say I'm not impressed."

He narrowed his eyes. She made it sound like he slept with any woman with a pulse, and then kicked them out of his apartment five minutes later. Yeah, he dated a lot, but one date didn't mean he automatically had sex with the woman. Lately it had been getting less and less. "Sure. Whatever."

She sighed. "I'm serious, Leo. This whole thing was cute when you were younger, but now it's a little strange. Carla is a great woman. An *older* woman, in case you didn't notice. I don't know if I approve of you getting your hooks into her, considering how long your...*relationships* tend to last."

He pushed up from the couch and walked across the room. Fierce, irrational anger twisted his gut into a knot. What right did she have to come in here and talk to him like that? He didn't want to blow up at her in her condition, but if she kept going he wouldn't be able to help it. He turned back to her, his arms crossed over his chest.

"Can you just make up your mind? One minute it sounds like you want me to date Carla, the next you're warning me to stay away from her. I give up. What is it you want me to do? God, I swear I need a roadmap to follow this conversation."

Alice's eyes widened and her lips parted. She blinked a few times before she answered. "I want you to be happy. And I want Carla to be happy. I just don't know if you should be happy together, or separately."

Women. He felt like tearing out his hair. Or hers. It wasn't her place to decide what happened between him and Carla, no matter how much she tried to butt her nose into his business. He couldn't wait for the baby to be born. Then she'd have someone else's life to run and she'd finally leave him alone. "Look, Alice. It's great that you want to think of Carla's wellbeing, but I have to tell you you're pissing me off. What Carla and I do is our business, whether you like it or not. If I want to pursue something with her, I will. I'm not a kid anymore, and I don't need your permission. I'll be damned if I'm going to let you, or anyone else, stand in the way of something important."

Since he and Alice had both inherited their father's quick temper, he expected a screaming fight. But she didn't scream. She laughed. "I knew it. You're in love with her, aren't you?"

Love? Shit. *No.* He clenched his hands into fists. All her complaints, all her anger. None of it had been real. She'd been baiting him the whole time. And he'd fallen for it. He should have known better. She'd tortured him this way so many times growing up, and he'd been stupid enough to let her dupe him yet again. "No. Of course not."

"Bullshit." She raised an eyebrow in challenge, daring him to deny it. "Go ahead. Tell me you're not. Just say no, Leo."

He opened his mouth to do just that, but the word wouldn't come out. *What's the problem? It's just a simple word. N-O. No.* "Yes."

Where the hell did *that* come from?

"Well, then." Her voice wasn't much above a whisper. "That changes everything, doesn't it?"

He swiped a hand through his hair, shook his head to try to get the world to make sense. What had he just confessed to? And why had he blabbed, to his sister no less, the first chance he got? He'd be lucky if she didn't run and tell Carla as soon as she left his apartment.

"Gee, ya think? I'm in a little bit of a mess here. Now if I could get her to notice me as a man instead of a kid she used to baby-sit for, my life would be just peachy."

Alice clicked her tongue. "No need to get all sarcastic. I want to help you."

Help? Yeah, right. He eyed her suspiciously. The last time she'd wanted to "just help", he'd ended up grounded for a week. Now he had a lot more at stake than losing TV for a few days. "How are you going to help me?"

"*If* you're serious about this—and Leo, you have to be *really* sure—I might know a way to get her to see you're for real."

He blinked at Alice, struggling for something to say. Did he want to trust his sister with something so private, so personal? He grimaced. The idea didn't hold a hell of a lot of appeal. But Alice and Carla had been close since grade school. Who better to help him find a way into Carla's heart than Alice? It was a delicate situation, one he couldn't afford to mess up, and his sister may have a viable solution. As much as he wanted to keep her as far away from his love life as possible, she'd offered him something the logical part of his brain wouldn't let him turn down.

"Hell yes, I'm serious. I've never been more serious about anything in my entire life." And it scared the hell out of him. The whole situation did. He hadn't even realized the depth of his feelings for Carla until Alice had tricked him into admitting it. He drew a deep breath and let it out on a frustrated sigh. "Okay, sis. What do I need to do?"

* * * * *

Carla's stomach growled as she walked through her front door. After work, she'd gone shopping to clear her head of all thoughts of Leo, whom she hadn't heard from since he'd sent the flowers three days prior. An hour at the mall had turned into four, and by the time she walked into the darkened parking lot it had been just after ten and the stores had all locked their doors for the night. In all her haste to discover the best sales, she'd forgotten to eat.

But despite her empty stomach, she felt better than she had in days. Why did she need to put her paycheck in the bank when she could have that cute little designer black dress? And the matching handbag. And the pumps. And that gold watch she'd had her eye on for months. Of course, the cut of the dress required purchasing new underwear so she wouldn't have a panty line, not to mention the new bra that would enhance her cleavage.

It had all gone downhill from there.

Okay, so she'd gone a little overboard. Just a tiny bit. She deserved it. She'd been so stressed for the past couple of nights that she'd barely had four hours of sleep. Total.

The lack of a decent night's sleep had led her to pick up the baby pink pajamas with red hearts all over them. Nothing like the feel of luxuriant silk to lull a woman to sleep. She didn't even want to think about the pillow perfume. Or the new sheets. Or the chamomile and vanilla scented candles to help relax her.

What the hell were you thinking?

She tried to laugh off the voice of reason, but it didn't want to go away.

Seriously, Carla. You haven't had a shopping binge like that in years. Haven't you outgrown the need to spend nearly all of your paycheck in one day yet?

Apparently not.

She dropped the shopping bags on the kitchen counter, glancing at Leo's flowers out of the corner of her eye. Looking at them made her want to pout like a five-year-old. Why hadn't he called? Was she that bad of a kisser that he didn't want to see her again?

That couldn't be it. He'd sent them *after* the kiss. If she'd been terrible, he wouldn't have bothered with what had to be at least a hundred dollars' worth of flowers.

So what had happened? There had to be something that had made him change his mind about chasing her. Had he meet someone else? Someone thinner, prettier? Someone *not* old enough to be his mother?

Well, okay, so she wasn't *that* old. But no one accused her of being a college coed, either. At least not in the past twelve years.

She sighed, flipped on the kitchen light and rummaged in the fridge for something resembling a meal. Five minutes later, sitting at the table with a bowl of reheated spaghetti and a glass of ice water, her mind drifted back to Leo. As usual.

She'd done a lot of thinking since her lunch with Alice. They'd spent a good deal of time talking about relationships while eating their meal. Carla might have hinted to her friend that her mystery man could possibly be a few years younger, and Alice had told her it didn't matter. She'd told Carla to go after what she wanted, and not to let a silly thing like a couple of birthdays get in the way.

Alice had also told her, practically in the same breath, to make sure he wanted the same things she did before getting too involved.

Talk about conflicting information.

But Alice's words had gotten her thinking. She'd done nothing *but* think in the past few days—about Leo, about her goals, about what she wanted from him, from life— and she'd finally come to a decision. She hoped.

Mapping out her goals was easy. She wanted a wedding. A big wedding with a church and a white dress and little girls throwing flower petals down the aisle. A husband who cared about her, treated her as an equal in all ways. A couple of beautiful, perfect children and a home with a white picket fence, four bedrooms, and a pool in the backyard. She wanted to work part-time, or even not at all, and spend most of her time raising her family.

But she wanted Leo, too. So bad she ached everywhere.

It had been a long time since she'd wanted someone the way she did him. She couldn't remember the last time a man had turned her inside out so effortlessly. He wanted her, too. He'd made that pretty clear with his actions last time they'd spoken. So what if it couldn't last. Did that really matter? Wasn't she entitled to one more fling before she started looking for her future husband? Okay, one single fling.

Yes. Assuming Leo's interest hadn't waned after the kiss.

She'd have to find out, without being too obvious about her intentions. She could call him, but what would she say? Somehow "Gee, Leo, you seem a little distant since you shoved me up against a wall and pushed your hands under my shirt" seemed a little too forward. And she couldn't call out of the blue. She'd never done that before. If she seemed too eager and he'd changed his mind, she'd make a total fool out of herself. If she hadn't already made a fool out of herself acting like a wanton ninny only to have him push her away before they made it to the bedroom.

Her gaze drifted to the flowers, and an idea formed in her mind. She smiled. *Perfect.* She really should have called him much sooner, but she assumed she would have heard from him after their little…incident in his apartment. Maybe he was waiting to hear from her first. A thank-you call was in order. Or, better yet, a little visit. Now, when he hadn't been home from work all that long, seemed as good a time as any.

Still smiling, she grabbed her keys and walked out of the apartment, shoved the keys into her pocket, crossed the hall and knocked on his door.

While she stood there waiting, the-pain-in-the-butt voice that lived in her head started wishing for him to not be home. She tried to snuff out the prayers, but to no avail. The voice wouldn't be silenced, and soon it got her nerves in an uproar. Her hands started to shake, and her knees trembled, just a little.

What had she been thinking, coming over here unannounced? How rude was *that*?

What if he hadn't meant to kiss her at all? What if it had just been a spur of the moment thing he now deeply regretted, and he never wanted to see her again? No. That couldn't be the case. He wouldn't have spent so much money on flowers for a woman he'd never see again. Would he?

Ridiculous, the whole situation. Had she been transported back to high school or something? She should just go home, write him a nice thank you card, and drop it in his mailbox like any normal, mature woman would do. Acting like some teenager wasn't going to earn her brownie points.

She didn't get the chance to leave. The door swung inward, and then Leo stood in front of her wearing a royal blue button down shirt, open from top to bottom, revealing a white undershirt stretched tight across his toned pecs. Her jaw dropped and she raised a hand to swipe at the drool that had to be coating her chin. With his hair mussed and his feet bare, he looked like she might have woken him from a nap, save for the fact that he held a wooden spoon in his hand and had a small checkered towel tucked into the waistband of his pants. Cooking? Leo?

He *cooked*? Really cooked, not just reheated things his mother made for him? He really had changed, a lot more than she'd expected.

"Hey, Carla." One corner of his mouth lifted in a purely male smile and he leaned a hip against the doorframe.

She gulped. "Hi."

"Did you need something?"

Yes, your body. All night long. She coughed. "I just wanted to thank you for the flowers. They're gorgeous."

His smile widened, even though a little wisp of disappointment flashed in his eyes. He shrugged a shoulder. "Sure. No problem. Anything else?"

Did he want to talk about the message on the card? A little shiver ran through her at the thought. "Listen, about that kiss…"

"Shh!" He put his finger to her lips and a spark flared low in her stomach. She almost darted her tongue out to moisten her suddenly dry lips, and touch his finger in the process, but held herself back.

"What's the matter?"

He dropped his hand from her skin and glanced over his shoulder. When his gaze returned to hers, guilt flashed across his eyes. "Nothing. I just have some company."

Someone he wouldn't want to know about the kiss. Or about Carla.

Another woman.

She tried to push the suspicions aside, but they wouldn't budge. Nothing else made sense. He didn't want her to meet his company, and he didn't want the company to know about her. He had to be seeing someone else.

What had she expected? He was a young, good-looking man in the prime of his life. He wasn't going to ignore other women just because he'd kissed her once. But she'd been hoping. Obviously a little too hard.

She narrowed her eyes, all the blood draining from her face and settling in the pit of her stomach. How could she have been so stupid to hope that more would come out of their relationship...well, the single, scorching kiss they'd shared?

"Um, thanks again for the flowers. I just wanted to let you know I appreciated them. Sorry I disturbed you from your company." Tears of disappointment threatened her eyes and she gulped back a lump in her throat. If she didn't walk away now, he'd see how upset she was, and she couldn't have that. She'd have to act like it didn't bother her that he could be sending her flowers, and then three days later be cooking dinner for another woman. And as soon as she got home she'd shred the bouquet and toss the remains into the fireplace. "I guess I'll see you around."

He grabbed her arm and pulled her to him, sealing his mouth over hers before she could protest. She wanted to fight, really she did, but when he kissed her like that she had no control over her impulses. She wrapped her arms around him and pulled him even closer.

He broke the kiss much too soon—like *two hours* too soon. Her body wept at the sudden loss of contact. But the sensual fog cleared, dropping her back to the real world with a bone-shattering crash. He had other, more important things to attend to. His *company*. She sent him an icy glare. "How dare you kiss me when you've got another woman waiting for you in the other room?"

He had the gall to laugh, the corners of his eyes crinkling in amusement. "Is that what you think? It's not another woman."

A woman's voice wafted into the hall from his apartment. "Leo, the sauce is burning."

"Go ahead and stir it," he called back, not taking his gaze off Carla.

How could he stand there and lie to her with such amusement on his face? Did he think she was dumb enough to believe anything he said? Maybe the other woman's voice was all in her imagination. *Not.* Her foot itched to stomp down on the top of his shoe.

"You can't lie to me. I'm not deaf or stupid. I know you've got a woman in there. I'm not going to be just one of the women you're seeing. This is exactly why nothing could ever happen between us. You obviously have a lot more growing up to do if you think this is okay. I think it's best if we forget that mistake of a kiss ever happened." She narrowed her eyes, ready to hiss and spit some more, when recognition hit. Her face flamed. *Oh crap.* "Alice."

"Yes, it's Alice. Jimmy's away on a business trip, and she was lonely tonight. So I told her to come over for a while."

"That's really sweet of you." *And I'm the world's biggest paranoid bitch.*

He pulled her back to him and planted a kiss on the top of her head. "I care about you, Carla. I would never do anything to hurt you. There are no other women in my life, please believe that. You know, you're cute when you're jealous."

She pulled out of his grasp and put her hands on her hips, hoping her expression at least resembled indignation.

"Jealous? What do I have to be jealous of? You and I don't have anything going on."

"Yet." His tone was so deep and smooth she almost had to grip the wall for support. His voice stroked her *everywhere*.

Alice's call from the other room interrupted anything Carla might have said. "Leo? The pasta is done. Are you coming back sometime tonight?"

Carla took that as her cue to leave before things went too far right there in the hallway. She backed up a step and offered him a weak smile.

"So…I'll talk to you later?" she asked, crossing her fingers behind her back. Hopefully her little tirade wouldn't chase him away.

"Oh yeah. Definitely."

She turned to walk away when he spun her around and pressed a hard, fast kiss to her lips.

"Have dinner with me," he whispered against her cheek. "Tomorrow night."

"Uh-huh," she mumbled, unable to manage more with his fingers digging into her hips. He released her, his gaze as heated as her face felt. When he stepped back inside his apartment, she drew a deep breath to clear her head. The air, filled with his clean, masculine scent, had the opposite effect.

"Great. I'll meet you at your apartment at seven. Wear something sexy, okay?" He winked before he closed the door.

She sank down against the wall until her butt hit the carpet. "Wear something sexy?" What kind of a man asked that of a woman on a first date?

The kind of man who knew how to get a woman's panties damp with just a few simple words. The kind of man who could kiss a woman senseless, and then do something so romantic as sending her a huge bouquet of wildflowers. The kind of man she wanted in her life, for so much more than a weekend fling. She sighed. It just wasn't fair.

She'd finally found someone she could see settling down with, but he was all wrong for her. In all her marriage fantasies, she'd never pictured someone like Leo. And she had good reasons for that. Too many to name. But now it seemed her mind, and her heart, had changed the fantasy. Hopefully one date with him would be enough to alleviate her temporary insanity, because she was doomed to a lot of pain if she thought Leo was The One.

Wear something sexy. Oh, she would all right. Thanks to her therapeutic shopping trip, she had just the right outfit. Leo thought he was in control. She laughed to herself. When he saw her in that black dress, he wouldn't know what hit him.

Chapter Six

ɶ

Whoever had mislabeled this *headband* as a dress ought to be arrested.

Why hadn't she noticed in the store fitting room that the thing had practically no back? It also ended halfway down her thighs — if she tugged at it every five minutes — and the neckline dipped so low she wouldn't be able to bend over all night. Not if she wanted to keep her breasts where they belonged. Inside the fabric.

She smoothed her hands down the front of the dress, only managing to wrinkle the soft, stretchy fabric. With a harassed sigh, she threw her hands in the air. Thirty-five-year-old women did not dress like nineteen-year-olds. At least the sane ones didn't. She could *not* go out of the house looking like this.

Hadn't there been a news story about fitting room mirrors and how they trick people into thinking they look good? Maybe she should have paid more attention. But, no. The store mirror trap had claimed yet another victim. She sighed again, grunted and tried to yank the dress down to meet her knees. One more useless impulse buy and the credit cards would have to go through the shredder.

She fished around in her closet, tossing slacks and skirts this way and that, but found nothing that caught her eye. Frustrated, she slumped down on the bed — or at least she tried to. The tight cut of the dress made sitting comfortably on the soft mattress nearly impossible. She should wear jeans and a T-shirt like she did when she went out with Steve. He could take his "wear something sexy" comment and shove it. Why bother getting all dressed up for some kid she'd known forever?

Because he didn't kiss like a kid.

He kissed like a full-grown man. A virile, powerful man who made her legs shake and the breath rush from her lungs with one kiss. *One kiss.* It took only something so small to turn her into a big ball of lust.

Pathetic, Carla.

She had to find something else to wear. If Leo saw her in the way-too-tight dress that did nothing to hide her flaws and made her look like she'd tried too hard to find the fountain of youth, he'd probably turn around and run before the date even got started.

It would serve her right, too, trying to dress like a teenager.

She pulled another pair of pants from the closet and held them up to her waist when someone knocked on her door. "*Damn it.*" She tossed the pants into the huge pile of already-rejected garments and rushed for the door. With her luck it would be Alice. Just what she needed — a lecture on top of everything else.

Giving the hem of the dress from hell one final tug, she swung the door open. But it wasn't Alice who stood there. Leo, ten minutes early, the jerk, stood in the hallway, grinning and looking amazing in a burgundy v-neck sweater and a pair of tight black jeans.

Oh man.

Her stomach bottomed out and all the moisture fled from her mouth to a destination further down her body.

Sure, she'd said it before, but with the way those particular jeans molded to his...package, he had to be the sexiest thing she'd ever seen.

"Sorry I'm early," he told her, his tone low and intimate. "I've been on edge all day. I just wanted to see you."

Sexy and sweet. Oh yeah. *That* would help her to resist his charms. She just smiled. If she spoke, her voice would sound embarrassingly like a squeak.

"You look amazing," he continued, stroking her up and down with just his gaze—and getting her as hot as if his hands had made contact with her body. Did he really expect her to get through this meal without jumping on him? If things kept going at this rate, there was no way that was going to happen. And if he kept looking at her like he wanted to have her for dessert, she'd give it five seconds before she forgot the date all together and dragged him into her apartment.

He reached out and grasped the strap of her dress between his thumb and forefinger, giving it a gentle pull. "This dress...wow, Carla. I'm at a loss for words."

And desperately in need of an ophthalmologist if he thought it was acceptable attire. "Are you kidding? I look terrible. I'm too old to dress like this. Can you give me just a few minutes to go and change?"

He smiled and shook his head. "Carla?"

"Yes?"

"Just say thank you." The look he gave her had her ready to cancel dinner and skip right to the goodnight kiss.

"Thank you." She cursed the breathless quality in her voice. Why did he affect her so strongly? What made him so special?

Everything.

"Much better. Now go finish getting ready."

When she returned ten minutes later, Leo took her arm and led her down the hall. "You *do* look fabulous, by the way, and if I hear you call yourself old again, I'm going to wring your pretty little neck. And then I'll kiss you and make it better."

She shivered at the thought. Whatever else happened, this promised to be one heck of a night.

* * * * *

Leo had chosen a quiet, out-of-the-way restaurant for his first date with Carla. *Date.*

With Carla. As much as he hated to admit it, he still felt a little too excited over the whole thing. Like a kid who'd found his dad's stack of dirty magazines. Here he sat, at one of his favorite Italian restaurants, enjoying a great meal with the woman of his dreams — and he wasn't even dreaming.

Now if he could keep his hands off her until they finished the meal, he'd be all set. When he'd told her to wear something sexy, he hadn't even imagined the little black number she'd chosen. Fantasy-inspiring. Incredible. It hugged her curves in a way that made his mouth water and his heart pound against his ribs. He'd never seen her in something so blatantly sexy. It did amazing things to his libido. He hadn't felt this out-of-control in years.

She tucked a lock of hair behind her ear before she dug into her meal, a calm expression on her face. At least she'd relaxed a bit since he'd picked her up. For a while there, he'd been worried about her passing out on the way down to the car. Did the situation make her uncomfortable, or was she just as anxious as he?

At the moment, he really didn't care. She was here with him, wearing something that could have passed for lingerie, her hair left unclipped to tumble down her back and her lips painted a fantasy-inspiring candy-apple red. He'd be lucky if he made it through the evening without going crazy. None of the insipid, giggling twits he'd dated even compared to Carla. She was classy, elegant, with just a touch of rebellion that had never gone away, probably due to her upbringing and her free-spirited parents.

He'd always envied her family, the carefree way they let her be what she wanted to be with no arguments. His mother hadn't spoken to him for weeks when he'd told her he wasn't going to follow his father's footsteps and go to law school. He'd almost given in, almost changed his mind just to make his mother happy, but as he sat across the table from Carla in the softly lit restaurant, he was glad he hadn't. He'd learned early to follow his own mind and not worry about what others thought. That knowledge would help him now, as he did everything in his power to win her over.

"So what made you decide to go into graphic design? I thought growing up you'd always wanted to be a painter," Carla asked in between bites of her pasta. Entranced with watching her lips wrap around the tines of the fork, he ignored the question.

"Leo?"

He rubbed a hand down his face, trying to get his mind out of the gutter. What would Carla think if she knew he'd been fantasizing about where he wanted to see those lips next? And it had nothing to do with dessert. At least not in the conventional chocolate cake sense.

Focus, Leo. Graphic design, not graphic sex. "I like art, I like to create, and computers are a big field right now. I figured it would be the best way to do what I want, and not have to worry about being a starving artist or anything." And he'd been able to do what he wanted and still make his mother happy by getting a great job with a big web design firm. She didn't worry so much now that she saw he could take care of himself—though she still pestered him about settling down and raising a family.

The bonus of having a regular paycheck helped. He still painted from time to time, but found he loved working with digital graphics programs just as much as oil paints and watercolors. Though the medium was different, the freedom to create was still the same. "I'm hoping to open my own design firm someday, but I want to get a couple more years in where I am first, learn the ropes."

He winced as the words left his mouth. He should have thought before he said something so stupid. The comment would remind her of their age difference—one of the subjects he'd already deemed as taboo until he got her used to the fact that he wasn't going anywhere. She smiled, and he let out a breath he hadn't known he was holding.

"You're very ambitious."

"Yeah, I guess." At least she didn't say "for someone so young". Though he read the words in her eyes.

"So why is it that no woman has snatched you up yet? You seem like a great catch."

"Because I've been waiting for the right woman. I refuse to settle for less than everything."

"Haven't found her yet, huh?"

His heart thumped to a stop, slamming against his rib cage before stilling completely. He sucked in a couple gulps of air, his gaze locking with hers. What he saw in her eyes fueled his need to be honest with her. Hope. Need. Everything he felt inside was mirrored in her gaze. His heart clenched. He couldn't wait any longer. It was now or never. Time to lay it all out in front of her, and let her do with it what she would. He leaned across the table, fixing her with a heated stare.

"Oh, I've found her. She's sitting right in front of me."

Carla, who'd been midway through a sip of wine, coughed, sputtering the red liquid all over the white tablecloth. She set the glass down hard, spilling a little more wine over the rim and swiped a napkin over her lips. "I dye my hair. To cover the gray."

He laughed and picked up his own napkin, dabbing some wine from her chin. "You're cute when you're trying to deny there's any attraction between us."

"Well, it's true. I do. I've been finding gray strands in my hair for a couple of years. You just graduated college three years ago. Doesn't that tell you something?"

Yeah, that she was making a big deal out of nothing. Ten years didn't mean anything in the grand scheme of things. If he'd been the one ten years older, would she still make such a big deal out of the age difference? Somehow he doubted it. His sister Lauren's husband was seven years older than her thirty-two, and no one said a word about that. They'd all supported her decision right from the beginning.

He brought Carla's hand to his lips and brushed a soft kiss across her knuckles. Her gasp brought a smile to his face. "Tell me you don't feel anything for me."

Her gaze clouded and her soft smile fell. "There's attraction, I'll give you that, but it's just sexual. Pursuing anything further would be a bad idea. Pursuing anything at all is a colossal mistake. We're not compatible."

She didn't really believe that. It irritated him that she still stuck to that story, even after all that had happened. He turned her hand over and stroked her palm with the pad of his thumb. "The way we fit together when we kiss, the way our bodies mold like they were made for each other… I have to say I beg to differ."

Carla's eyes widened and she shook her head. "You might want to save this conversation until after the meal. I'm liable to choke on my food and need the Heimlich maneuver."

"Okay. I'll stop. But you have to admit we're good together."

She pulled her hand away and busied herself fiddling with the dessert fork next to her plate. "Again, that's just physical stuff. Emotionally, we're not on the same level."

He closed his eyes for a second and blew out a harsh breath. What gave her the right to assume that? She didn't know him very well if she still thought he was some teenager always looking for the next party. He was twenty-five, not nineteen. He had plenty of friends who'd settled down and started families. And even though he didn't consider himself ready for *that* much of a commitment, he had to admit he'd thought about it once or twice in the past couple of years. More since he'd given up on short flings and started pursuing Carla.

"Again, I think you're wrong."

"Please. The other night, when we met up in the hall, I'd been on a date with a man just about my age that had teenage children. One in college. You're still at the age where you want to party, have a good time. Enjoy your life. Me, I passed that a long time ago. Now I want more out of life." Disappointment flashed across her eyes, along with an aggravation that rivaled what had twisted his stomach in knots.

Time to change the subject before they ended up in an argument. There would be time later to convince her. Now he just needed to keep from screaming out that he wasn't the man she so obviously thought he was. "So how's the job? You've been working at Scarlet for, what, four years now?"

She smiled, her expression relieved. "Yep, four years last month. It's been great so far."

"That's good to hear." She pulled her hand out of his grasp and tugged at the thin little straps of the dress and, just like that, his focus shifted back into more sensual territory. Specifically, what she was — or wasn't — wearing under it. Given the cut of the dress and tightness of the fabric, it couldn't be much.

He turned back to his own meal, intent on making it through at least the restaurant portion of the date without reaching under the table to find out what kind of panties a woman wore under a dress like that.

"The food is good here."

He smiled at Carla's sincere words. "I'm glad you like it."

"Do you bring all your dates here?"

He nearly groaned. Not this again. When would she let this go? "No, Carla. Just the important ones." *Just you.*

What would it take to make her understand what she meant to him? He reached for her hand again, snagging her fingers with his. A jolt of heat ran up his arm and he had to force himself to stay seated. Her lips parted and she gulped. At that moment, the depth of his feelings and desires for her rose in his throat, threatening to choke him. *Shit*. Why hadn't he seen it before? It went beyond lust, beyond love, into foreign and decidedly scary territory. When she looked at him like that, he was ready to promise her the world. He dropped his hand from hers and went back to eating.

How was he supposed to handle this new development? And how could he possibly be feeling so much, so soon? It didn't make sense. Granted, he'd known her for his whole life, but he hadn't really known her at all until recently. His mind reeled and his mouth went so dry gulping down his whole glass of wine did nothing to ease it.

Carla touched his hand. "Is everything okay, Leo?"

"Yeah. Fine." But it wasn't. And now he had a lot of thinking to do.

"Are you sure?"

He paused with his fork halfway to her mouth, glanced at her with wary eyes. "Yeah. I'm sure."

Her smile, bright and honest, made him believe that everything would be okay. His tensed muscles relaxed and he put his emotions out of his mind. For now. Surely they'd come back and haunt him as soon as he was alone again.

* * * * *

The conversation hardly lulled through the whole meal, which surprised Carla. There had been that one rough spot when they'd almost finished their meals, when she'd seen something in his eyes that had scared her. Apparently, it had scared him too, because he'd backed off the subject of relationships mighty quickly, turning the conversation toward the upcoming birth of Alice's child instead. But once that awkward moment had passed, they'd slipped back into the easy banter they usually enjoyed around each other. Not many men could make her feel that comfortable on a first date. They talked right through dessert, and even the car ride home about life and work and sports and even cartoon shows, and she got to know him better than she'd ever thought possible.

She liked what she learned.

A lot.

Maybe too much, since a tingle had started in the general region of her heart around the time she finished her chocolate cake, and she couldn't get it to fade away no matter how much she tried to remind herself of what a bad idea it was to get attached to the guy.

She did *not* need this right now. She'd promised herself that Leo would be a fling. A *fling*, not some kind of great love affair.

The use of the "L" word in connection with Leo made a shudder race down her spine. Truth was it would take next to nothing for her to fall. He was everything she'd ever looked for in a man—smart, funny, kind, so sexy he made her mouth water.

The more she got to know him as a man, and not the kid she'd always thought of him as, the more her heart swelled. They got along great. They had more in common than she would ever have thought possible. He treated her better than most men had, but didn't make her feel like he was just trying to impress her by showering her with attention. Everything he did seemed genuine. Like he really cared. He'd be perfect for her.

If he'd been born a few years earlier.

She sighed as they stopped in front of her door. Time to say goodnight. Funny, but she really didn't want the night to be over. She'd gone into the date hoping for a quick little fling, a couple nights of great sex and an amicable parting. Now she wanted a lot more. She'd wanted sparks. She'd gotten them in spades. Forget just sparks. Being with Leo was like being struck by lightning. Nothing would ever be the same. *Ever*. The thought both thrilled her and scared her at the same time.

When she took her keys out of her purse, he took the key ring from her hand and unlocked the door, pushing it open for her. The position put him so close behind her that, when she turned around, she bumped the top of her head on his chin. He grunted, a grimace on his handsome face.

Good going, idiot! Why don't you break his arm while you're at it?

"Oh, Leo, I'm so sorry. I didn't mean to… It's just, I didn't know you were so close. I never would have —"

He shushed her with a finger to her lips, sending a sliver of heat knifing through her embarrassment. "It's not your fault. It's mine. I shouldn't have been standing right behind you. I can't help it, though. I love the way you smell. I can't get enough of you."

"Oh." She shivered, her legs going numb. His breath brushed her shoulders, his hands skimmed her hips, and if he didn't kiss her right that second she was liable to burst into flames and set off the sprinkler system.

She smiled. The landlord would frown on that sort of thing. Not wanting to get evicted, she wrapped her hand around the back of his neck, stood on her tiptoes and planted a kiss on his lips.

Her actions had the desired effect. He groaned and kissed her harder, pulling her tight against him. His hands fell on her bare back—maybe the dress had been a good choice, after all—his palms searing her skin. And still, he wasn't close enough. His tongue traced the seam of her mouth in a silent plea and she obeyed, parting her lips. His tongue thrust inside, possessive and greedy. She reciprocated eagerly but long before she cared for it to happen her common sense made her break the kiss and pull out of his arms.

Don't rush this, Carla. You have plenty of time to decide if he's what you really want. And she would need all of that time to resolve the dilemma clogging her mind. Did she follow her heart and see where this thing between them would take them, or did she follow her mind and push him away now, before he had the chance to break her heart and sour her for relationships for years to come? Years she didn't have, not if she planned on having children in this lifetime. She wasn't getting any younger. Forget the fling. It just wasn't going to happen, know matter how much she might want it to.

"Goodnight, Leo."

He stared at her, his eyes glazed with arousal. A slow, somewhat pained smile spread across his face. "Goodnight."

He dropped a small kiss on her cheek—sending her pulse skittering all over again at the intimacy of the simple act—before he walked to his own door. He unlocked it and stepped inside, turning and leaning against the doorframe.

The goofy grin she'd always loved was back, though it seemed a little strained around the edges. "I'm not shutting my door until you shut yours. Go inside and go to bed. I'll call you tomorrow."

"You'd better." She stepped into her apartment, hoping he didn't notice how much her body shook, and closed the door. Once safely inside her living room, she flopped down on her stomach on the couch and buried her head under one of the throw pillows. She'd gone into the date expecting one thing from Leo, but gotten so much more.

Why had she not noticed how great a guy he'd grown into? And now that she knew the truth, how was she supposed to keep herself from falling in love with him?

* * * * *

As Leo walked through his darkened apartment, not even bothering to turn on any lights, Alice's voice echoed in his head. "Don't be too forward. Take her out to dinner, talk with her—I mean really get to know her, Leo, no talking about fishing and motorcycles and stupid computer graphic programs she has no interest in—and let her make the first move. You've got a better shot at something lasting if you let her take control, at least at first. Take it nice and slow, or she'll think you just want sex."

He made his way into the bedroom and dropped onto the bed, covering his eyes with his arm. At that particular moment in time, with his heart still pounding and his cock fighting to break free from his jeans, he couldn't form a single coherent thought that *didn't* include sex. And Carla. And sex *with* Carla.

Man, he needed a cold shower—or three. At this stage in the game one wouldn't be sufficient. Hell, a hundred wouldn't even have the desired effect.

He wanted more than sex with her, but he couldn't tell her. Not yet. Tonight, she'd treated him like an equal rather than a nuisance—a big step, but he still had a little further to go before he could confess everything to her. Before he was even ready to hear it himself. Soon, he would tell her how he really felt. For now, though, he'd let her call the shots, even if it killed him. Leaving her tonight had just about done him in.

After a few minutes of lying in the dark, he came to the conclusion that the hard-on had no intention of going away on its own. With a pained groan, he forced himself off the bed and went into the kitchen, grabbing a beer out of the fridge. He opened it and chugged half the bottle in a gulp, hoping the cool, bitter liquid would cool some of his rampant lust.

Yeah, right.

Only one thing would tamp down his raging hormones. Carla. *But not tonight.* He stalked into the living room and flipped on the TV before he slumped down on the couch. He finished off the rest of his beer while he watched some inane sitcom, not able to focus on anything. *Let her be in control? Some advice, Alice. Look where it's gotten me.*

With any amount of luck, following Alice's advice wouldn't lead him to let Carla take too long to move their relationship to the next level. He needed to show her how good they could be together before she changed her mind. First, he'd take care of the physical side, and then he'd work on her emotions. Soon he'd get her to see that they were meant for each other, even if she had been born a little too soon.

Chapter Seven

ഔ

"Carla, break time is over. Your four o'clock is here."

Carla snapped her gaze to the doorway, where her boss Nikki stood brandishing a pair of scissors. She pointed them toward the wall clock and shook her head, laughter in her eyes.

"Okay, thanks." Carla stretched her arms over her head as she stood up from the plastic chair, stifling a yawn. "I'll be right there."

Another hour and she'd be able to go home and take a nap while she waited for Leo's call. Assuming he actually did bother to pick up the phone and dial her number. After she'd sent him packing last night—probably more than a little aroused—she'd be surprised if he wanted to see her again.

But she'd done what she had to, under the circumstances. He told her he was ready for the same things she was, and she intended to find out if that was true. She had thought a fling would satisfy her urges, but it wouldn't be enough. Casual sex went against her makeup, no matter how much she tried to force herself into it. If he was as ready for more than a casual fling as he said, spending a few nights alone before they fell into bed together wouldn't chase him away. And if he left, chose not to bother calling again, she'd know she would be better off without him.

Why did that idea hold about as much appeal as having her bikini line waxed?

"Hey, you okay?" Nikki asked, a frown marring her pixieish features. "You don't seem like yourself today."

Carla picked up the book she'd been reading and stuffed it back in her bag. "Yeah. I'm fine."

Nikki's smile widened, turned conspiring, and she flipped her long, dark hair over her shoulder. "Okay, then. If you say so, I'll have to believe you. But if you want to talk about it, you know I'll listen." She winked. "Hey, speed it up a little. Cameron is waiting."

Carla rolled her eyes, an automatic reaction to hearing Cameron Murphy's name. Leo's friend. The one who had inspired such jealousy in him. The guy came into the salon way too much—at least every three weeks up until a month or two ago—to get his hair trimmed. Flirting seemed to be a part of the guy's nature—he couldn't turn it off. Like most people needed to breathe, Cameron needed to flirt. Normally she wouldn't mind—even welcomed it when her prospects seemed so limited—but since he was a good friend of Leo's she dreaded facing him that afternoon.

She walked out of the back room and found Cameron leaning against the front counter, laughing and joking with Shelly, the nail technician. Doing exactly what a man his age should be doing. *Having fun.* Watching him with Shelly made her question yet again her decision to see Leo. Shelly had just turned twenty-one last week.

Carla shook off the old woman blues and walked over to them, pasting a sappy—and very fake—smile on her face. "You ready, Cameron?"

He didn't attract her the way Leo did, but looking at him she understood why everyone envied the fact that she got to be the one to cut his hair. She smiled as she took in his lean, athletic build, his light brown hair, and bright patterned tie that served as the only splash of color against his white dress shirt and black pants.

"Whenever you are." He followed her to her chair and sat without even a hint of his usual teasing manner. What was that all about?

"How are you today?" she asked as she draped a cape over him and started wetting his hair down with a spray bottle.

"Good. And you?" He smiled at her in the mirror, but his expression seemed a little tense. *Strange.* He'd never acted this way around her—or any other woman in the salon—before.

"I'm fine." *I think.* Though feeling a little stuck in the *Twilight Zone.* Had he suddenly noticed that everyone else who worked in the salon was young, and she wasn't? Any other day, he would have answered with some juvenile comment, like "You sure are". And any other day, she would have answered back with "Call me in a few years, when you're older". But not today. Though she wasn't as upset about his odd behavior as she would have been on a different day.

She didn't know what Cameron's problem was, but hers could be defined in one word. Leo. She had to face it. She was hopelessly stuck on the guy. Ever since the first time he'd kissed her. It wouldn't be something that would go away, either. Even if he decided one date had been enough, she wouldn't be able to let him go as easy.

As if reading her mind, Cameron asked, "So…you and Leo, huh?"

He startled her so much she dropped her scissors. And then her comb. Her fingertips went numb. What had Leo said about them to his friends? "Um, yeah. I guess." She grabbed a new pair of scissors and a comb.

"Too bad. I might have asked you out, but I'd never go after another guy's girl."

Girl? She snorted. She hadn't been someone's *girl* since the tenth grade. She straightened, glanced in the mirror and caught him checking out her butt. Her face flamed. Evidently, the secret guy code that wouldn't let him openly flirt with her didn't cover ogling her when he thought she wasn't looking.

Several times during his haircut she caught him looking at her. A small smile touched his lips. His piercing green eyes, amused and knowing, had her wanting to run in the other direction. She didn't want anyone finding out about Leo, especially her coworkers. She'd never hear the end of it. What had she done to deserve the attentions of not one, but two men in the prime of their lives? Maybe switching to that new perfume a few months ago had been a wise decision after all.

A giggle threatened to escape her throat, but she held it back. "You do realize I'm thirty-five, right?"

His eyes widened. "No way. I mean, I knew you were older, but I didn't think you were *that* old. Wow. You're really hot for a chick your age."

"Gee, thanks. I think." Did she have "baby magnet" tattooed across her forehead?

"I didn't mean it that way. I just meant that you look twenty-eight or twenty-nine. Maybe thirty at the most.

You've aged very well." He shook his head just as she closed the scissors over a lock of his hair, making her cut a piece in the back too short.

"Hold still or you're going to end up looking like I did your hair with a lawn mower." *And stop talking while you're at it. You're making me nervous.* "So, Leo mentioned me?"

"*Mentioned* you? He never shuts up. You're all I hear about anymore."

She smiled, her insides going all mushy. Her face probably flushed a thousand shades of red. "Really? Cool."

Oh, lovely. Not only did she date much younger men and dress like a twenty-year-old, now she'd started talking like one.

A wide smile stretched over Cameron's mouth. "Yeah, really. Just, ah…remember what I said if you two don't work out. You can always give me a call if you need a shoulder to cry on."

She bit back another very juvenile giggle. "I will." *Yeah, right.* Though his attention flattered her, he wasn't the kind of man who would interest her. He acted like a twenty-something man should act—young, single, carefree. So unlike the way Leo seemed to be. Maybe she and Leo weren't that different, after all. Perhaps whatever had sparked between them that night in the laundry room might lead to something intense, lasting. Permanent.

Yeah, and she might wake up in the morning with the body—and mind—of an eighteen-year-old. *Fat chance.*

She finished up with Cameron, said goodbye, and went to work on her last client of the day, her downstairs neighbor, Mrs. Phelps, who came in to have her hair colored every couple of months. The woman had been coming to Carla for the past year, and assured her that she trusted no one else with her delicate locks.

Big mistake.

The first hint that something had gone wrong came as Janie, the assistant, rinsed the hair color from Mrs. Phelps's hair.

"Um, Carla?" she called, a nervous look on her face. When Carla walked over to the sinks, her eyes widened. Mrs. Phelps hair had turned pink.

"Nothing to worry about," she whispered to Janie. "I'm sure it'll turn the normal auburn shade when it's dry."

It didn't. Drying only made the pink stronger. The poor woman looked like she'd stuck her head in a cotton candy machine.

Nikki, who walked by as Carla tried to flatten the fluffy pink strands with a pick, dropped the bottle of hairspray she held in her hand and gaped. "What did you do?"

"That's an unusual shade, dear," Mrs. Phelps said, running her fingers through her short, curly hair as she squinted into the mirror. "What is it called?"

Baby Doll Pink. A shade popular with much younger clients who enjoyed spending their weekend nights in trendy dance clubs. Never before used on grandmothers who were presidents of their garden clubs and made quilts for all the expectant mothers in the neighborhood.

A groan welled in Carla's throat. She was *so* dead. Nikki would kill her as soon as she got her alone. She'd skin her alive—and not without reason. Mistakes like this just couldn't be allowed to happen in this business. She pushed her hand through her hair, her stomach tightening into a painful knot. She had to make this right. But how?

Nikki winced and shooed Carla away from the woman. "Yeah, you know what, Mrs. Phelps? I think the bottles were mislabeled when they came to us from the company. This isn't the color you usually get. If you just give me a few minutes, I can fix it for you. Your visit today will be free of charge, as will all the others until we fix your hair the way you originally wanted it to be."

Mrs. Phelps shook her head. "No, I think I like this fine. I've always enjoyed seeing the younger people with all the bright colors on their heads. Besides, maybe it'll shock my husband, Marty, enough to get him up from in front of the TV and out getting some exercise."

Carla grimaced. Somehow the image of Marty Phelps and his conservative ways didn't mesh with his wife's new, outlandish look. At least the hair color—just a temporary rinse—would wash out in a week or so. That was probably the only thing that saved Carla from losing her job. She would have quit from sheer mortification if she hadn't needed the steady paycheck to support her retail therapy habit and her taste for four-dollar pints of ice cream.

After Mrs. Phelps paid for her *interesting* new 'do and left the salon, Nikki pulled Carla to the side of the room, an aggravated yet amused expression on her face. "What is wrong with you today?"

"I'm sorry. I wasn't paying attention."

"You know, I'm trying really hard not to laugh at this. It *so* isn't funny, yet I can't get the picture of little, frail Mrs. Phelps with pink hair out of my mind." Nikki shook her head. "You're never like this. I don't know what your problem is, but I think you should go home. You've been out of sorts since you walked in this morning, and it's obviously not getting any better. You need more rest, or medication, or something to calm down your nerves."

Carla tried to argue, but Nikki wouldn't hear it. She waved her hand in the air and glanced around the salon. "Your shift is almost over, anyway, and your appointments are done. There really isn't too much point in you hanging around. Kylie and I will clean up tonight. You can owe us each a night closing. You go home before you wreck my salon."

Not one to dispute the obvious truth, Carla got her things and left the salon, driving the short distance to her apartment building in a daze. What was wrong with her? She'd never done anything that stupid before. Ever since sending Leo away last night, she couldn't seem to wrap her mind around a full thought. Something had to give. Maybe her best option would be to get Leo out of her system before she did something *really* serious, like total her car or burn down her apartment building. Once she'd relieved some of her stress, maybe she'd be able to concentrate.

* * * * *

Leo couldn't believe his luck. His day had been amazing, his hard work landing him two new accounts for the company. Wanting to share his good news, he'd been planning to visit Carla around the time she usually got home from work. But she'd beat him to it. When he swung his apartment door open, she stood there looking frazzled and cute and absolutely loveable. Given his euphoric emotional state, he did the only thing that came to mind.

He pulled her inside, slammed the door, and kissed her thoroughly.

When he finally broke the kiss, they were both panting.

"Did you need something?" he asked, hoping she hadn't stopped by to borrow a bottle of floor cleaner or something else that would make him look like a complete ass for hauling her inside the way he did.

She just smiled. "You."

Nothing had ever sounded sweeter. His body rejoiced and a primal scream threatened to erupt from his chest. He held it back, pulled her tighter against him and placed a soft, urgent kiss on her lips before he let her go. "Good."

His gut tightened, his erection pressing firmly against the front of his pants. This was what he wanted—a woman like Carla to come home to after a terrific day. He took her hand and led her to the couch, pushed her back so she fell to the cushions. Within seconds he was on top of her, his body pressed against the softness of hers, his lips sealed to hers in a searing kiss that had him rock-hard in seconds. He'd never known anything so perfect in his life. If she pushed him away again, his heart would stop beating and his body would explode.

She devoured his mouth, her hands all over him. Her legs wrapped around his waist and his erection pressed tightly against the juncture of her thighs. He groaned at the feel of all that heat so close, separated from him by only a few layers of fabric. His fingers fought to free her of her shirt, to bare her to his eyes and his touch and his mouth.

Without warning, Carla shifted, knocking them both off the couch. Leo landed on the floor between the couch and coffee table, flat on his back with Carla on top of him. He groaned long and loud, his erection straining against his zipper.

"Oh God. I'm so sorry." Carla winced, obviously misreading his groan. When she started to climb off him, he gripped her hips to hold her in place. Which caused her to squirm. The squirming nearly caused him to lose it in his pants.

"Stop moving so much. *Damn it.* Hold still for a second." Or else he might prove her wrong about being man enough for her. He helped her strip out of her shirt and was working on the button of her pants when he halted, unable to go any further. What a time for chivalry to invade. "Shit. Carla, we can't do this."

Carla, who had just shoved her hands up under his shirt, whimpered. "Why not?"

Yeah. Why the hell not? Because he'd been raised better than that. As the only two men in a houseful of women, his father had made sure Leo learned how to treat a lady right. Carla wasn't someone he'd picked up for a fling. She was so much more. "Not here. I don't want our first time together to be some frenzied screw on my living room floor. You deserve candles, roses, silky lingerie. You deserve a bed, at the very least. This isn't going to happen tonight, sweetheart. I won't do that to you when I could give you so much more than this."

She snorted. "I don't need you to do anything to impress me. Believe me, Leo, I'm sufficiently impressed. Forget the roses and the candles, and the uncomfortable nighties. Just take me to bed."

Okay, chivalry only lasted to a point. When a sexy woman all but demanded a guy take her to bed, no man in his right mind would refuse.

She stood and he followed, scooping her up in his arms and carrying her to his bedroom.

Once inside, he kicked the door closed and dropped her on the bed. She bounced a little on the mattress before settling back and propping herself up on her elbows, laughing. "Okay, Caveman, what do you have planned now?"

Oh, so many amazing, delicious, tantalizing things he'd been waiting years to try with her. In all the time he'd waited, bided his time, he'd developed an extensive list of things he'd do should he ever get her in this position. His fingers itched to touch her, his tongue begged to taste the sweetness of her skin. And he would. Many, many times. And she would love every second.

"So many things. I wouldn't even know where to begin to explain it all to you."

"Oh, yeah? Try."

"First, I'm going to make you come so many times you forget your name."

Her laughter died and her eyes widened.

"And that's only the beginning." He stripped off his shirt and climbed into bed beside her.

Chapter Eight

ରେ

Carla's breath caught in her throat and she couldn't think of a single thing to say in answer to his bold statement. He planned to do *what*? Make her come *how* many times? A full body shiver raced through her at the thought. Had any man ever made her an offer so tempting?

Not in this lifetime.

"Lie back and close your eyes," he whispered, his breath tickling the bare skin of her neck.

She shouldn't let him get away with acting like such a domineering barbarian, but for the life of her, she couldn't remember why. Had she really ever thought she'd have to be the one in charge in bed? That he wouldn't have a clue as to what he was doing and she'd have to teach him everything? How wrong she'd been. Leo had turned into a take-charge kind of guy. Her arousal ratcheted up another few notches. She flopped back on the mattress and squeezed her eyes shut. Waiting and anticipating. How did he intend to accomplish his goal? She couldn't wait to find out. Her body was strung so tight she might snap at any minute, but she didn't mind. If he made good on his promise, it would all be worth it.

After what felt like an eternity of lying flat on her back with her eyes closed, she began to wonder if he'd taken a good look at her body and left the room. "Leo?"

"Hmm."

Well, at least he hadn't run away screaming. "What are you doing?"

"Looking." His deep tone hit her right where it counted, dampening her panties and clenching her stomach. "Admiring. Deciding where I should start."

She opened her mouth to give him a few pointers, but his chuckle made her snap it closed again. "Patience, Carla. We've got all night. You just relax and let me take care of you."

All night? Her stomach flip-flopped. He could really go all night? As in from now until the sun came up again? Maybe there was something to this younger man thing after all.

His warm fingers touched her skin, right below her rib cage, drawing a gasp from her throat. He traced lazy patterns on her abdomen and circled her navel, leaving a trail of goose bumps in his wake. She clenched her hands in the comforter to keep from grabbing him and pulling him down to her as instinct dictated. Waiting for more was sheer torture—but such sweet torture that part of her never wanted it to end. He blew a hot breath across her skin that sent her pulse skyrocketing. Just when she thought he'd never touch her with anything more than his fingertips, she felt the warm wetness of his tongue across her stomach.

"You're wearing too many clothes." He laughed, the sound thick and rough with desire. And then his fingers went to work on her bra. Thank God for front clasps. Cool air rushed over her breasts as he freed them from the confines of the soft fabric, pebbling her nipples and sending a shudder through her.

"God, you're gorgeous. Perfect. Just how I knew you'd be," he murmured just before he closed his mouth over one beaded nipple. Her back arched almost of its own volition and her eyes snapped open. Leo, gazing at her intently, smiled without taking his mouth off her body. She darted her tongue out to wet her lips, enthralled with the dark, aroused look in his eyes. Had she really ever thought of him as a child? As too young to satisfy her? Now worry filled her — worry that *she* wouldn't be enough for *him*.

By the time he moved on to her other breast, her body teetered on the edge, ready to explode. If he didn't touch her where she really needed him to, and soon, she might do just that. She tangled her fingers in his hair and tugged until his head lifted from her body.

"Leo, please." She cursed herself for sounding like a lust-ridden maniac. Leo didn't seem to care. In fact, he seemed to like it. A sensual smile played at the corners of his mouth and his gaze darkened even further. He trailed a line of hot, wet kisses from her chest down her abdomen, stopping just above the button on her pants. She wriggled under him, trying to get him to move down, just a little further. He took the hint.

Within seconds he had her pants unbuttoned and he slid them down her legs, taking her shoes off with them. At least she'd had the foresight to wear the sexy red bra and panty set. She would have died had he caught her in the awful white granny ones that had caused her so much embarrassment that night they ran into each other in the laundry room.

"Nice," he growled, lifting the elastic on the waistband of her panties and letting it snap back into place. "They have to go."

Hearing the frustration in his voice, she couldn't resist a little torment. "But you said we have plenty of time."

"Yeah, that was five minutes ago." He slid back up her body and kissed her hard before he drew her hand to the front placket of his jeans—where his impressive erection swelled below the fabric. "Things have changed a little."

She sat up and rid herself of her bra, watching his eyes the whole time. He looked like she felt—hot and bothered and ready to blow at the slightest provocation. The fact that she had that effect on him filled her with power. She smiled at the thought, fought against a giggle threatening to break free.

"What's so funny?" He raised an eyebrow, pushed her back against the mattress.

"I was just thinking how cute you look all aroused."

"Aroused? Sweetheart, that's a gigantic understatement." Without warning, he reached down and grasped the waistband of her panties again. With a swift tug, he tore the material from her body. The sound of ripping elastic and lace filled the air and she gasped, more from the sudden rush of arousal the action caused than his action itself.

"What are you doing? Those were my favorite pair."

"I thought you said the white ones—"

"Don't even go there." She pulled him down for a kiss, eager to distract him from anything that might take away from the moment—like her sheer, utter embarrassment over the white granny panties incident.

She skimmed her hands down his bare chest while his mouth worked wonders on the sensitive skin behind her ear. He took her earlobe between his teeth and gave it a gentle tug. A low moan escaped her lips and a shiver raced down the length of her spine.

"You like that?" he asked, his tone unbelievably husky.

"Umm," seemed to be the most coherent sound she could form. Anything more than that was too much for her lust-ridden mind to handle.

It got worse when he pushed her legs apart and skimmed his hand up the inside of her thigh. His fingers gently parted her folds, one dipping into her sex. "You're so wet. So ready for me."

Nothing like pointing out the obvious. "Why don't you do something about it?"

"Oh, I plan to." He swirled his finger around her most sensitive places, sending sparks shooting through her lower body. She moaned and thrust her hips up to meet his caress. It didn't take more than a few seconds before she felt her belly tighten with impending orgasm.

"Leo, you've got to stop. I'm so close."

He didn't make a move to stop, only smiled. "I know."

"I want you inside me."

"What did I tell you?" he asked, his tone filled with laughter as he pressed his fingers harder. "Come for me, Carla. Let me watch you let go."

She wanted to hold back, to have him buried deep inside when she spiraled out of control, but she couldn't hang on any longer. Her climax rushed over her, sending her into waves of pleasure until she shattered in his arms.

She closed her eyes and let herself drift. Leo's jagged breathing filled her senses, the heat of his skin so close to hers, the electricity in the air arcing between them as her body and mind floated along on the most delicious sensations she'd felt in too long to remember. The bedsprings creaked as he stood up, and only then did she open her eyes. "Where are you going?"

"I need to have you. Now. Be right back." He left the bedroom and returned moments later, a box of condoms in his hand. He tossed it onto the bed next to her and started to strip off the rest of his clothes.

She picked up the box and turned it over in her hand. Brand-new. Never opened. *Family pack.*

Oh man.

Leo came back and kneeled on the bed. He took the box out of her hand and ripped a hole in the side, shaking out a single packet. Once he'd sheathed himself, he settled between her parted thighs. But he didn't enter her, not right away. He kissed her, hard and insistent, as he caressed as much of her skin as he could reach. He was everywhere all at once, his hands and lips and tongue, playing on her every sensitized nerve. Dragging her along on the most exciting ride of her life.

When her body started to climb again rapidly approaching the boiling point, she nipped his lip. "Please, now, Leo."

"Yeah. Now." He fitted himself against her, running his erection over her folds in a teasing manner before plunging into her sex. Once fully seated within her, he held her hips to still her movements.

She reveled in the feel of him buried so deep. It felt right—like nothing had ever felt before. It was the most perfectly exquisite sensation in the world, and she wanted to remember it always. Deep inside her mind, in a place she refused to acknowledge, she knew she'd found everything she'd been looking for—right here in Leo. She couldn't ask for more.

Except, maybe, that he move.

She wrapped her legs around his waist and dug her heels into his rear, uttering an unintelligible moan. He laughed, took the hint and began to thrust. With each rhythmic stroke of him inside her, she felt herself spiraling higher and higher, getting closer by the second to the peak of climax. He lifted her hips and angled his thrusts just a little, and pushed her over the edge into another explosive orgasm. She grabbed fistfuls of his hair, her legs tightened around him and she cried out in intense pleasure.

Leo followed not long after, stiffening above her as his climax racked his body. He collapsed on top of her, his ragged breath hot against the side of her neck and their sweaty bodies entwined.

Myriad emotions filled her in the charged silence. Satisfaction, shock, elation, and the urge to do it again. Soon. Just to see if the first time was a fluke, of course.

When her breathing had returned to normal, she smiled at him. "I can still remember my name, you know."

One corner of Leo's mouth crooked into a devilish grin. He leaned down and kissed the tip of her nose. "Now you're just asking for trouble."

She pinched his arm. "Nope. I'm just reminding you that you haven't fulfilled your promise."

"Not yet." He ran his fingers down her cheek, his gaze heating again. "There's still plenty of time. You're not getting out of this bed all weekend. We have a lot of lost time to make up for."

Oh boy.

* * * * *

Carla woke up slowly, every muscle in her body thrumming with a delicious ache. She stretched her arms over her head and yawned, enjoying the feel of utter and total satisfaction.

Four times.

They'd made love four times during the night.

The muffled sound of the shower running down the hall registered in her sluggish mind and she debated going to join Leo. In the end, she decided to wait for him to come back to her. Once they got all dirty again, she'd insist he take another shower. *Then* she'd join him and see to it personally that every inch of his delectable body got clean.

When he came into the bedroom a few minutes later wearing nothing but a towel and a smile, she patted the mattress.

He frowned. "I thought I'd make us some breakfast."

She shook her head, feeling amorous and not willing to let him ignore her. He brought out something in her that no one else had managed to find — something wanton, insatiable, and she'd be damned if she let him walk away without giving her a chance for a little fun first. "Come here." She crooked her finger and he came, smiling slyly.

"What do you have in mind, Carla?"

She reached out and yanked the towel off, wrapping her hand around his length. "Are you always this hard in the morning?"

"When I have a beautiful woman waiting for me in my bed, I am."

He said the sweetest things. "If I'm counting correctly, I think I'm one up on you in the orgasm department."

Leo made a noise that sounded like a combination of a whimper and a growl. "If you say so. I mean, I hadn't been counting or anything, but who am I to argue with a statement like that?"

"Smart man." She leaned in and took him in her mouth. He groaned and tangled his hands in her hair, his fingers digging into her scalp, bordering on the edge of pain within minutes. Arousal knotted her stomach and dampened her bare sex. She had a sinking suspicion they were going to miss breakfast.

* * * * *

It was well past lunchtime when they finally made it out of bed. Leo cooked a quick meal and set the table for two. Carla surprised him by sitting in his lap.

"If you sit there for long," he told her, "I'm gonna want to take you to bed again. I don't think either of us would survive another round. At least not this soon. Not for another few days, at least." Though the idea sorely tempted him.

"You're probably right. We'll just eat. For now." She smiled down at him, lifting a forkful of pasta from his plate and bringing it to his mouth. He took the food, swirling his tongue around the tines of the fork as he did so.

The woman was insatiable. It seemed she had more stamina than even he, a man ten years her junior, did. Not that he planned to complain about that. He'd give Carla anything she wanted, even if it killed him. Which, if they kept going the way they'd started, it might. He smiled to himself.

At least he'd die a happy man.

"What are you smiling about?" she asked, offering him another bite of the spaghetti with spicy red sauce. She took a bite for herself while he answered.

"Do you know how beautiful you are?"

"I have doubts, but you seem insistent on telling me." She set the fork down and broke off a piece of bread, bringing it to his lips. He took it—and her fingers along with it—into his mouth and sucked it out of her grasp. She pulled her fingers from his mouth. Slowly. Making his cock harden against the front of his sweatpants. He chewed and swallowed, not tasting the food but tasting Carla on his tongue instead. A shiver racked his body and his mind started to fog. *Stop. Not again. Neither one of you will be able to walk for a week.*

"I only speak the truth. You're beautiful, incredible. Like no one I've ever met. Last night was... Hell, it was amazing."

She nodded, her expression taking a serious turn. "So where do we go from here?"

The caveman in him wanted to claim her as his, never let her leave his apartment again. But the more sensible, modern man who usually overrode his baser impulses told him not to rush things. If he told her that he loved her so soon, she'd run away screaming. Or she'd tell him to stop lying. Or she'd laugh in his face. With none of those options holding much appeal, he went for the safer, and slower, route. "How about dinner tonight?"

She smiled. "Okay."

"And the night after?"

"Sure."

"And what about the night after that?"

She nodded.

Relief flooded him. This was going to be the beginning of a wonderful—and very intimate—relationship.

He'd tell her how he really felt, in time. For now he'd let her get used to the idea of the two of them together. If things went well, after a few weeks he'd be able to confess his real feelings. With any luck, by that time she'd reciprocate. And *then* he'd ask her to move in with him. If all went well after that—

Stop it, man. You're looking way, way too far into the future.

And it scared the hell out of him. But at the same time, he couldn't wait. Everything would be perfect. He didn't see it turning out any other way.

Chapter Nine

ഗ

The shrill ring of the telephone jolted Carla out of a deep sleep. She yawned, rubbed her eyes, and ran her hand along the bedside table until she found the receiver. She stifled another yawn as she lifted it to her ear.

"Hello?"

"Carla? It's Anne. Did I wake you?"

Her eyes wide, she bolted into a sitting position. This was *so* not good. "Um, no. Of course not."

She glanced at the clock. Eight a.m. Since when did she sleep so late?

Since she'd started seeing a man who knew a few tricks to keep her awake and interested all night. She hadn't made it to the gym more than once this week, and it was all Leo's fault. She smiled at the thought. Last night had been amazing. The most wonderful night of her life, all thanks to Leo.

And now she had his mother on the phone.

Not a good situation.

"I was wondering if you were free for dinner tonight. Lauren and her husband are coming down for the evening, so I thought it would be nice to get the family together."

Oh man. Dinner with Leo's family? And most likely Leo, too? Now that would be an uncomfortable situation. But she didn't dare turn it down—then she'd have to explain to Anne and Alice why she couldn't make it to the meal.

Leo's lips brushed the center of her back, trailing lower down the length of her spine. She spun around and shook her head.

"Who is it?" he asked, his tone rough from sleep.

She put her finger to her lips and made a shushing sound. "Your mother," she mouthed.

He laughed. *The jerk.*

"Carla? Are you all right?"

"I'm fine, Anne." She narrowed her eyes at Leo and shook her head. "Dinner sounds terrific. Do you need me to bring anything?"

"Alice mentioned you're seeing someone new. Why don't you bring him along?"

Carla choked. Yeah, *that* might happen. "Um, I think he has to work tonight. I'll have to come alone."

"That's too bad, dear. I was really looking forward to meeting your new man."

You already know him. Quite well, actually. "Another time."

"Absolutely. We'll see you around six?"

"Sounds great." Sounds like the most uncomfortable situation in the world. "I'll see you then."

"Oh, and Carla?"

Leo's fingertips brushed her bare breast and it took all her willpower not to whimper. "Yes?"

"Have you seen Leo lately? I tried calling him last night and this morning, but I got no answer."

His hand trailed lower, settling on her stomach before dipping even further down. She gulped. "If I see him around, I'll tell him to give you a call."

"Thanks. I'd appreciate it. I want him to be there for dinner, too. I'll see you tonight."

Carla hung up the phone and glared at Leo, trying to bat his hands away. "Stop touching me for a second. This is serious. It's nothing to fool around with. Your mother just invited me to dinner."

One shoulder lifted in a casual shrug. "So?"

"So she wants you to call her so she can invite you, too."

A slow, amused smile spread over his lips and he flopped back onto the mattress. "Well, I guess it's about time everyone finds out about us. It's been a week. Obviously this isn't a one-night stand."

Her stomach clenched at his words. Was he out of his mind? One single week didn't equal lifetime commitment. "No. You can't say anything to anybody about us. Especially not your family."

He frowned, his expression thoughtful—and a touch guilty.

"Wait a second. You haven't told them yet, have you?"

"No, but I don't see why we shouldn't. " He propped himself up on his elbows, all hints of teasing gone. "What's your issue with this? We're together. Why do you have such a problem with people finding out? Are you embarrassed by this? By *me*?"

"No. Not at all. I just don't think it's something we should be broadcasting."

"Tell me, Carla. Do you always keep your relationships a secret?"

"No."

He sighed. "Just this one, huh? Fine." He climbed out of bed and started pulling on his clothes.

"What are you doing? Leo, where are you going? Come on. Knock it off. Think about it for a second and you'll realize I'm right. This isn't even a relationship."

He spun on her, his gaze searing and his stubble-lined jaw tight. He held his hands out in front of him and shook his head. "It isn't? Then why the hell am I wasting my time here? See ya, Carla."

He grabbed his shirt and shoes and strode from the room.

Anger, along with a little fear, flooded her. He wouldn't really walk out on her, would he? Not over something this trivial.

Not if she had anything to say about it.

She jumped up, wrapped the sheet around her, and followed him to the door. Her fingers encircled his arm and she tried to tug him back toward her. He swung the door open before he turned and glared. "What?"

"Don't do this. Don't leave. Please."

Tears welled in her eyes, but she didn't understand why. This relationship couldn't last. Too many things stood in their way. But it didn't stop her from hoping that maybe, just maybe, she'd found something different in Leo. It stung like hell when he shook his head and walked out the door. Her stomach knotted, but her legs froze in place. Instead of following him down the hall, she leaned against the doorframe and called out to him.

He turned back, his dark expression softening just a little. "What now?"

"Come back. Please. I'm so sorry."

Sadness tinged his smile, and he shook his head. "Not now. Maybe later. I need some time to think. And you know what? You do too. I think we both went into this expecting different things, and maybe we need to reevaluate it all before we continue with anything. I'll see you tonight, Carla."

He unlocked his door and disappeared into his apartment without giving her a chance to reply. She stepped inside and shut the door, leaning against it and sinking down to the floor. If this was just a fling, something that had no lasting potential, why did she feel like she was coming apart inside?

It's the newness. It'll wear off in time.

Even though the more logical part of her mind accepted that as the truth, her stubborn heart refused to believe. Leo was special, and she'd never find another man like him.

But that didn't make everything all right.

* * * * *

Leo smoothed his hands down the front of his charcoal gray dress shirt before he opened the door and walked into the house he'd grown up in. Carla was already here. Her car sat in the driveway, along with Alice and Jimmy's SUV and the new sports car George had just bought Lauren for her birthday. Gina, his perpetually late sister who swore that she planned to ignore her thirtieth birthday next month, would probably arrive with her latest fling in tow.

But where was Sophie? When he'd spoken to his mother, she'd assured him all his sisters would be there. Sophie, at twenty-six, had always been closest with him. She'd moved an hour away when she'd gotten married, but she and Mack always managed to bring the kids down for family dinners. Tonight, especially, he needed to talk to someone who would understand.

He walked through the large, open foyer into the kitchen to find his mother standing by the stove, her long, dark hair pulled back into a neat ponytail and an apron covering her light blue dress. Alice and Carla sat at the kitchen table, Carla with a glass of wine and Alice with what he guessed to be water. His mother ran over to give him a hug. Alice smiled at him, but Carla glanced at him with uncertainty etching her beautiful eyes.

He couldn't resist. Though he knew it would upset her, he gave her a quick, heated smile. "Hey, Carla."

His mother raised an eyebrow, but said nothing. Her actions didn't surprise him. She'd known for years about Leo's crush on Carla. She just didn't know it had gone so far past the crush stage. And, if Carla had her wish, she'd never know. *No one would.*

Anger spiked through his stomach. The idea that she wanted to keep their relationship secret twisted his gut in knots. Was she ashamed of him? Of them, and what they'd done? He was ready to announce it to the world, and she wanted to keep it buried in the closet like some dirty secret. He gritted his teeth, but pasted on a sappy smile.

Her gaze searched his, uncertain and wary, before she returned his smile with a weak one of her own. She stole a glance at Alice before she turned her attention back to him. "Hi, Leo. How have you been?"

He caught the underlying question in her tone. How had he been since he'd walked out on her that morning. The worry in her voice threatened to tear him apart. She cared, even if she refused to admit it. One of these days, he'd get her to open up. But not tonight. Though he wouldn't be able to stop himself from trying— unobtrusively—throughout the meal.

"You know. Same old thing." He fixed her with an intense stare—until his mother cleared her throat.

"Leo."

He swung his gaze in her direction. "Yeah?"

"Nicky and Sarah are in the living room with Sophie. They've been asking for you all night. Why don't you go say hello?"

He smiled. He could take a hint. Leave Carla alone before he said something stupid and chased her away. If only they knew. This time next year, maybe they'd have an announcement to make. But until then, he'd do as she wanted and try to pretend he hadn't spent most of the night before pounding into her. "Yeah, okay."

He patted Alice on the head as he walked by, heading toward the entrance to the living room. "Hey, kiddo. How's it going?"

"Kiddo? I was practically a teenager when you were born."

Well, damn. Did she have to say something else to remind Carla about the age difference between them? He leaned in to whisper in her ear. "I thought you were on my side here?"

Alice smiled. "Love knows no sides, little brother. Keep that in mind."

His mother and Carla gave them curious stares, but kept silent. For that, he was grateful. He'd have to speak to Alice about her secrecy skills when he got her alone. "Is Jimmy here?"

She nodded. "He's out in the living room with everyone else. I think they're watching some kind of sports thing."

Her words brought a smile to his face. "A sports thing, huh? Is Gina here yet?"

His mother shook her head. "She was supposed to be here a little while ago, but you know Gina. She goes by her own clock, and not the ones the rest of the world uses."

"What about Sophie? She's here, but I didn't see her car out front."

Alice coughed. "Yeah. She's here. For a while."

"What do you mean?"

"I'm getting a divorce."

He glanced toward the doorway to see Sophie standing there, a glass of wine cupped in both hands and a solemn expression on her face. The breath flew from his lungs and he shook his head. "Excuse me? What did you just say?"

He had to have heard her wrong. Sophie and Mack had been married for the past seven years—since they were both nineteen. Even then they'd known what they wanted. Each other. And they hadn't let anyone talk them out of their dreams. Now, seven years and two children later, they were splitting up?

"Mack…" She let out a deep sigh and shook her head. "We haven't been happy for a while, Leo. We've decided it's best if we go our separate ways. That's why the car isn't here. I don't have it anymore. I still have to look into buying a new one, since I told him to take the one we used to share."

"A divorce? Why didn't you say something?"

"I didn't want to bother anyone with it. Not until I was certain we couldn't work things out." She offered him a weak smile and tucked a glossy, dark brown curl behind her ear. "Why don't we go sit down and talk? Mom, Alice and Carla have already heard the story. I don't think I want to bore them with it again."

"Yeah. Okay." He gave Carla a quick glance before he followed Sophie out of the room.

She walked out onto the back porch and slumped onto the wooden steps.

He followed, sitting next to her and leaning his elbows on his knees. "Tell me what's going on, Sophie."

She heaved another sigh, filled with aggravation and defeat. "He wasn't happy. He said we got married too young, and that he hadn't known at the time what he really wanted. Apparently, what he really wanted wasn't me."

"How can that be possible?" Sophie was the kindest, sweetest woman he knew. How could Mack not want such a wonderful woman? Any man would be lucky to have her as a wife, as the mother of their children. "What did he do, Sophie? Did he cheat on you?"

A single tear slipped down her fair cheek. She ignored it. "Um, yeah. He did. But it's okay."

Anger rose in his throat, threatening to choke him. When he got his hands on Mack, the man's face would never be the same. "How can you possibly think it's okay for him to be with another woman, when he pledged his life to you?"

"We hadn't been happy in a while. *I* hadn't been happy. I'd been looking for a reason to end it, and his affair gave me the perfect one." She offered him a small, sad smile, but hope flared in her eyes. "It's going to be fine, Leo. Really. I'm happier now than I've been in years. Though it's an adjustment being back here with Mom and Dad, the kids are happy. We're going to be fine. I've registered them for school, and I plan to go out and look for a job once they get settled."

He clenched his hands into fists. Fine? Hah. It didn't sound like it to him. "Is he helping you with the kids? He's not going to leave you to do it all by yourself, is he?"

She shook her head. "He's going to come visit them on weekends. Take them overnight sometimes."

"Good. I'd have to kick his ass if he didn't." He pushed a hand through his hair. "Whatever you need help with, honey, just ask. Whether it's money, or babysitting, or finding Mack and making him do his fair share—whatever you need, or want, just ask. You know I'll be there for you."

More tears shone in her eyes, and she brushed them away with the tips of her fingers. "Thank you, Leo. That means so much to me. Maybe once in a while you could take Nicky out to play ball? He's going to miss that, with Mack so far away."

"Absolutely. You just let me know when."

What the hell was the world coming to, when the two people he thought were as happy as his parents couldn't keep it together long enough to hit their ten-year anniversary? He let out a deep breath. This *sucked*. Nothing else could describe how he felt about the whole thing. They'd been too young, she'd said. Nineteen. What did that say for him and for Carla? Was he really too young to settle down and make a commitment?

"Enough about me and my sad state of affairs. What's going on with you lately? Mom said you're seeing someone new?"

Her tone of voice told him she wasn't surprised. He laughed softly. How many times had he brought women home to meet his family? Too many. He'd hoped to bring Carla as his girlfriend tonight, but maybe she had the right idea. No sense disappointing everyone if they weren't even sure it could last.

"Yeah, there's someone."

Sophie's smile lit up her whole face. "I can see in your eyes that she's special. I'm glad you finally got over that stupid crush you had on Carla long enough to find a woman that makes you happy."

He scrubbed his hand down his face. What was it going to take to get *someone* to take him seriously? "My *crush* on Carla is not stupid."

Sophie blinked at his outburst. "Wow. So what does your new woman think about your little obsession?"

"She's fine with it." More than fine, if the way she screamed herself hoarse the night before was any indication.

"Oh, really?" Sophie shook her head, took a sip of wine and turned her attention to the yard. After a few moments she swung her gaze back to him. "You know, Leo, I've never presumed to tell you how to live your life before, but it isn't going to happen with Carla. She's in a different place in her life, looking for things you aren't ready for. You still have a lot of years to live. Don't be like

Mack and try to tie yourself down so soon. Live a little first."

He'd lived plenty. Enough to know that there wasn't another woman out there who satisfied him like Carla did on so many levels. "Yeah. I think I'm all set with the whole living thing. I'm six years older than Mack was when you got married. I think that counts for something."

"Yeah, it does. But you've been hung up on Carla for so long that you haven't given any other woman a fair chance. Do that, before it gets to be too late." She put her hand on his arm. "So what's your new girlfriend's name, anyway?"

He debated for all of two seconds before he decided to tell her the truth. She might not agree with his decision, but she might. It would be nice to have someone else on his side through this whole mess. And maybe she'd have a few suggestions to get Carla to admit their relationship in public. "Carla."

Sophie clicked her tongue. "Come on now, Leo. Now you're even dating women with the same name?"

"No."

"What do you mean?" A frown marred her features before her eyes widened in understanding. "No way. Don't tell me that you and Carla are seeing each other."

"Almost every spare minute."

A wide grin broke out on Sophie's mouth. "No *way*. I don't believe it. You and Carla? Carla Michaels?"

Why was that so hard to believe? He frowned. "Yeah. Is that a problem?"

"No. I didn't mean it like that. I just… I never imagined she'd return your interest."

"I can be very persuasive when I want to be."

She held her hand up in front of his face. "Stop right there. Anything further would fall under the TMI heading in a major way. But are you happy?"

He let out a breath on a long sigh. Yeah, he was. But would it last? He kept waiting for the other shoe to drop and everything to crumble down around him.

"Your hesitation makes me worry." She patted his shoulder. "Please don't let my situation dampen your happiness."

"I'm not."

"What's wrong? You're worried for other reasons?"

"Well, yeah. I'm trying like hell to be confident about this, but there seems to be so much standing in our way. She doesn't even want to tell anyone we're seeing each other. It sucks."

"Give her time. Whatever you're feeling, I'm sure she's feeling it too. Keep that in mind. It's a little strange, I've got to tell you, to find out that you're sleeping with Alice's best friend. But I'll get used to it. We all will. Just give her the space she needs and everything will work out."

Says the woman who's in the middle of a divorce. "I'm sure it will."

He shook his head. Even he was starting to not believe it. Everything was too terrific, too perfect. It couldn't last. Could it? He didn't know anymore. But he'd do everything, *anything* in his power to make sure it did.

Chapter Ten

ॐ

Leo leaned his elbows on his thighs and let his head droop. Sophie had left him alone outside, telling him she needed to check on the kids, but he couldn't bring himself to go back into the house yet. His sister's news still shook him. Why hadn't he seen it coming? Why hadn't any of them in the family? Sophie hadn't said a word, but they had a big family. Someone should have picked up on the signals that something wasn't right. But apparently, none of them had, and now Sophie was miserable. She didn't say she was, not in so many words, but he saw it in her eyes. Mack had hurt her more than her stubborn pride would let her admit. Leo fumed, his hands clenching into fists.

Fists he'd like to bury in Mack's face.

Rick Spencer had raised his son right. Men didn't cheat on their wives. The ones who did were scum, lowest on the earth. Women should be treated with respect, and it pissed him off that Mack had done something so wrong to his sister. But he knew Sophie well enough to know she wouldn't appreciate him going after Mack. And she didn't need to deal with Leo's anger along with her own pain, so he'd have to keep his mouth shut and his hands to himself, no matter how much it killed him to do it.

Divorce hadn't been something his family had ever had to deal with in the past. He came from a long line of happily married couples. His parents, his grandparents, aunts and uncles…up until now, divorce had been something that other people did. And Sophie wasn't one to give up easily. She fought for what she had, even if everyone told her it was wrong. It must have gotten really bad with Mack for her to walk out and take the kids with her. But she'd done it, she'd stood up for herself, and he was proud of her for that.

At least with her living closer, he'd get to see his niece and nephew more often. He'd meant what he said to Sophie. Whatever she needed, he'd do. And if Mack decided he no longer wanted the responsibilities of being a parent now that he had a new woman in his life, Leo would personally see to it that Mack was there for his kids, and for Sophie money-wise, no matter what it took.

His thoughts drifted to Carla, and the way he felt about her. His feelings were strong. More than strong. But would it be enough to keep them together? Maybe she was right. Maybe this wasn't something they needed to share with the world, because it might not be something that would last. If she was already this nervous, this hesitant, there were no guarantees that she wouldn't bolt a year or two down the road. He couldn't see investing that much of his time, his life, in someone just to have them walk away. But people did it all the time. What drove them to marry when half of them would just end up divorced?

Carla's face, her laugh, and that air of innocence she had floated through his mind and he smiled. That was what made people do it. Finding that one person who made you complete. Made you want to commit not only to a relationship, but to making yourself a better person. Carla did that to him. She was it.

But he wasn't about to be stupid and rush into anything.

Sophie's marital problems had shown him what a mistake that would be.

Something told him it wouldn't be like that with Carla, that she'd be permanent, but he ignored it. There were no guarantees in life, and he wasn't going to take any chances. Especially when she was so bent on pretending the emotions between them didn't exist. All along he'd been so sure, so certain that she was the woman for him. But even so, did anything really last forever? He wanted her in his life, but what would guarantee she'd stay there?

He tried to push away the niggling doubts, but they wouldn't budge. Suddenly nothing seemed as sure or as certain as it had been before he'd talked with Sophie. His life, his thoughts had been turned into a jigsaw puzzle that had been taken apart, and he didn't know if he had the patience to put them back together again. He and Carla were right together. They fit, in all ways. But would that really matter in the end?

He could tell himself over and over again that things would always be perfect, but the truth was, he didn't know. Nobody knew what life had in store for them. Now he just had to decide if the uncertainty would be worth all the trouble.

* * * * *

Carla found Leo sitting on the back steps, staring out into the darkness. He didn't look up when she stepped out onto the porch, didn't even show any signs that he knew she was there. His gaze remained fixed straight ahead, his elbows on his knees and his hands clasped in front of him. His shoulders slouched, his back heaving with his deep breaths. Her fingers itched to reach out and touch him, to make sure everything was going to be okay, but she shook off the urge and took a seat beside him, not too close so they didn't attract unwanted attention from his family.

She reached her hand out to touch him, but pulled it back before she made contact. "Dinner's almost ready."

He didn't even look at her. "Thanks. I'll be inside in a few."

"What's the matter with you?"

He sighed, shook his head. "Did you know Sophie and Mack are getting a divorce?"

Was that was this was about? He was upset because his sister was getting a divorce? He couldn't be this sullen over that, could he? Sophie actually seemed happy about it. Carla had taken the news to mean she'd finally managed to break away from what had apparently been a stressful relationship. Her husband had cheated on her. She deserved so much better than that, and Carla applauded her decision to leave. "Yeah, I heard something about that. Is that what has you so thoughtful right now?"

He shrugged.

"Leo? Talk to me. You've never had a problem opening up to me before."

"Yeah, well I guess that was before I knew where I stood with you." His shoulder muscles bunched, pulling his shirt tight across his back. "But you made it perfectly clear this morning where I stand in your life."

What was his problem tonight? He'd shown up happy, teasing everyone and taunting her. Now his mood had soured to the point that she didn't want to be around him. And he was going to pin it all on her? Not if she had anything to say about it.

"What's that supposed to mean?" Aggravation knotted her stomach. She clenched her hands into fists, closed her eyes for a moment before she slid him another glance. "Well? Are you planning to answer me sometime tonight?"

He stood and walked across the yard, out of sight among the trees and the darkness. Not a word to her, not even a glance over his shoulder. He was *so* not getting away with that. She pushed up from her perch, and followed.

When he stopped a few feet in front of her and turned abruptly, she almost ran into his back. "Hey! Give a person a little warning, will you?"

His eyes flashed in the pale light of the moon. His jaw tightened and he shoved his hands into the pockets of his pants. "Tell me one thing, will you, Carla? Why are you so worried about what everyone else thinks?"

"Who said I was worried?"

"You didn't have to say it. I understood when you told me to keep *silent* around my family."

Men. Did they always have to be so dense? When would he see that she was doing it for his own good, as well as hers? His parents didn't need to know what was going on between them, and neither did his sisters. It would make things so much easier that way. Now if she could just get it through his thick skull. "I'm trying to protect you. I don't want you to get uncomfortable around your family once this ends."

His gaze hardened even more, his mouth drawing into a thin line, and she realized her words might have been a mistake. To a guy like Leo, her explanation may have sounded like a threat to his ego. She braced herself, waiting for him to blow up. He didn't disappoint.

"*Protect* me? You've got to be kidding me. The last thing I need from you is protection, Carla."

Without warning, he pressed her up against the nearby fence, pinning her body between the rough wood and his firm, muscled body. A shiver ran down the length of her spine and settled into a flutter in the pit of her stomach. She swallowed hard and tried to duck out of his grasp, but he wouldn't let her go.

"You don't have to worry about me, Carla. I'm a big boy, sweetheart. I can take care of myself. Right now, you're the one who needs protection."

Another shiver washed over her, more intense than the last, and her knees nearly buckled. "What do I need protection from?"

A small, strained laugh escaped him. "Me. In about two seconds I'm going to rip this pretty little dress off you and show you exactly what I'm feeling right now."

He didn't even give her a chance to reply to his bold comments. He leaned in and crushed her lips with his, spearing his tongue between her parted lips. The kiss seemed to go on forever, him taking more and more of her with each stroke of his tongue, each press of his fingers into the soft skin of her hips. His body pushed her harder against the fence and her fingers flew to his shirt in a mindless attempt to push him away before they were caught—or to pull the garment from his body before she melted into a heap of useless lust on the soft grass.

He broke the kiss and pressed his lips to the side of her neck. "I need you, Carla. All the time."

"But here… We can't…"

"Just let me touch you for a little while." He kissed her again and her common sense took a vacation. His lips were so perfect, his body such an amazing fit against hers. Everything about him fit her to perfection. *Everything.* The more time she spent with him, the closer she came to admitting the truth to herself, if not to him. The thought of another man, a boring, stable one, held no appeal for her anymore. How could she settle down with someone else when the man she wanted was standing right in front of her?

Troubling thoughts, but they'd have to wait to be analyzed. Right now her mind was too busy trying to fight off the sensual fog, so thick that the footsteps coming up alongside them barely registered in her sluggish brain until someone cleared his throat.

"Leo, your mother asked me to tell you dinner is ready."

Leo broke the kiss and stepped back, turning to face the man who'd spoken. "Dad."

Rick Spencer stood a few feet away, his burly arms crossed over his chest, a look of blatant amusement on his face. He let out a hearty laugh and shook his head, his gaze shifting from Leo to Carla and back again. "If you two are busy, I can always make up some kind of excuse."

Carla gulped, trying not to meet Rick's eyes. Funny, but she'd known him so long she felt like she might get into trouble for getting caught making out with his son in the backyard.

Knock it off, Carla. You're thirty-five, not fifteen.

But Leo was still a kid.

No, he isn't.

She sighed. If she had to admit the truth, she didn't think of him as a kid anymore. Not in the least. Every time he touched her, her body went up in flames. And he knew, *really* knew, just what would turn her on. He hadn't even had to ask. Leo was no fumbling kid. Not even close. He was a fullgrown man—one who apparently had more sexual experience than she did. A lot more.

That was an unsettling thought.

"Are you okay, Carla?" Rick asked concern heavy in his voice.

She nodded, not trusting her voice. Her face flamed and she wanted to duck through the gate, run to her car, and hightail it out of there before it got any worse.

"Dad, how about we don't mention this to Mom."

Rick laughed, much to Carla's surprise. "Don't worry. That won't be a problem. I wouldn't want her hounding Carla like she hounded Tina and Rachel."

A frown tugged at the corners of her lips. What had happened to Tina and Rachel? And why did both men shiver at the mention of the names in conjunction with Anne?

Rick nodded, shifting his gaze from Carla to Leo and back again. "Okay, then. I'll see you two inside in two minutes, right? You know your mother, Leo. If she thinks something is wrong, she'll come out searching for you herself."

"Yeah." Leo's tone sounded a little nervous. "We want to keep this quiet, so I'd appreciate it if you kept everyone in the dark, as well as Mom. We'll be right behind you."

With a smile and a nod of his head, Rick turned and headed for the house. Carla watched him step through the back door before she sank against the fence and let out a heavy sigh.

"You okay?" Leo asked, turning around to glance at her.

"Fine. That was pretty painless, huh?"

Leo laughed. "Yeah, right. I'm sure I'll get a dozen lectures later, starting with the 'keep it in the bedroom' one. He just didn't want to embarrass you, but believe me, I know that look." He held his hand out to her. "Let's go get some dinner."

She slipped her hand into his and he gave her fingers a little squeeze. "So, tell me about Tina and Rachel."

He groaned. "Why did I know that would be the first thing you'd focus on?"

"Because I'm a woman. In situations like this, we're a little prone to jealousy." She laughed and shook her head. "Seriously, I'm just curious. Could it really have been that bad?"

"Depends on your outlook." His fingers tightened around hers, sending a warming jolt up the length of her arm. "Tina was the first girlfriend I ever brought home to meet my parents. I wasn't serious about her, not in the least. I was only nineteen at the time. But that didn't stop Mom from bombarding her with never ending questions and dropping hints about how she'd like to see me settle down, eventually, with a woman like her."

Carla bit back a laugh. She'd known Anne to do things like that with her daughters' boyfriends as well. "Sounds horrific."

"Trust me. It was mortifying." He leaned in and dropped a quick kiss on her cheek. "Tina never wanted to come back to my parents' house for dinner again. And it was the last time I brought a woman home to meet them. Until Rachel."

The tone of his voice led her to believe things had been a lot more serious with Rachel than they had with Tina. An arrow of jealousy pierced her insides, sending a twinge of pain through her heart. She swallowed hard and braced herself for the story she was sure she didn't want to hear. "Who's Rachel?"

"A woman I dated a couple of years ago. I'd just finished college, so naturally my mother thought that would be a good time for me to start thinking about settling down. She set me up with Rachel, the daughter of one of her friends. Things might have gone well, if Mom hadn't butted in at every turn, trying to mold the relationship into what she thought it should be." He sighed, ran his free had through his hair and faced her with a lopsided smile. "I was never really all that interested in Rachel, but my mom kept pushing us together, hinting around that she'd like to see me start a family and all that crap I had no interest in at the time. It made me resent Rachel and what we had going, and I think the whole situation really hurt her."

"I'm sorry." She said the words, though she didn't feel the least bit apologetic.

"I'm not." The smile grew, turning sensual in the natural light of the moon and the artificial glow of the spotlight that illuminated half the backyard. "If she'd pushed me into marrying one of them, I'd be miserable right now instead of happy with you."

She frowned. The words sounded sincere, but forced at the same time. Was he having doubts? Had he finally come to his senses and decided he didn't want her in his life after all? The thought left her cold.

"Are you okay?" His fingertip came up, smoothing the crease between her eyebrows. "You don't look so good right now."

He wouldn't want to hear about her silly little insecurities. They hadn't promised each other forever, so what was her problem? She shouldn't be this jealous, this upset over something that was only temporary. He wasn't in it for the long haul. Neither was she.

But she wanted to be.

And she'd have to get over that. Fast. She had no future with a man like Leo. His stories had proven that to her better than anything else had in their short relationship. The man had all but said he had no interest in commitment. To wish for anything long-term — or even forever — between them would be emotional suicide. She was right in keeping their involvement a secret. That way it would hurt less when they inevitably decided to go their separate ways.

"I'm fine." She forced a fake, probably way too bright smile. "Just tired. Someone's been keeping me up so late at night that I may need to take a day off just to catch up on my sleep."

Leo chuckled. "Want me to beat him up for you?"

"Nah. I kinda like having him around." Loved having him around, but she'd never tell him that.

"Good, 'cause I have a feeling he plans to stick around for a long time."

He couldn't mean that. He wouldn't have said something so revealing. Yet when she looked up into his eyes, she saw nothing but sincerity in his gaze. Sincerity and affection. Maybe she'd been wrong about thinking he couldn't commit. She'd just have to wait and see.

Leo glanced toward the house. "Maybe we should head inside now, before they send out a search party."

"You're probably right. Couldn't have that happening."

They walked across the yard in silence, but the feel of her hand enclosed in his large, strong one made a warm tingle start low in her belly. Not a sexual feeling, but a comforting one. She hadn't thought much about it when it had happened, but he'd done something unexpected. He'd asked his father to keep silent about what he'd seen. For a man who'd practically been begging her to tell the world about their relationship, he'd been very careful to ask his father not to say a word. She smiled and squeezed his hand.

"Why did you ask your dad not to tell anyone?"

He didn't answer until they stood on the porch. He dropped his hand from hers. "Because you asked me not to."

That couldn't be his only reason. There had to be some ulterior motive. Maybe he'd finally come to realize that keeping their involvement from his family would be better for everyone. "But I didn't expect... I thought you didn't want to keep it a secret."

"I don't. But you do, and that's what's important here. One of these days, everyone is going to know and you won't be able to hide anymore. But for now, I'll do as you've asked me to, and keep my mouth shut about it. But only in public, Carla. In private, you're all mine." He placed a soft kiss on her cheek and stepped through the door into the house, leaving her standing on the porch all alone, her heart fluttering from his words and his actions.

This was the first time she'd seen a side of Leo that went beyond the sensual nights they'd shared.

No, that wasn't true. The night he'd made her soup for her headache and massaged her sore feet. The way he took care of his sister when her husband was out of town and she didn't want to be alone. His concern over Sophie's divorce.

He'd shown her his sensitive, caring side on many occasions, but up until tonight she'd chosen to ignore it. To take it for granted. Tried to convince herself that he couldn't possibly be mature enough for anything more than a one- or two-night stand.

But that was far from the truth.

Leo was kind, caring, and noble, strong, smart, and sexy. Everything she wanted in a man—in a partner to share her life with. And all this time she'd tried to tell herself he wasn't worthy of the future she'd planned for herself.

Maybe *she* was the one who wasn't worthy of *him*.

* * * * *

Leo shot a glance at Carla across the table, nearly laughing at her warning look. He couldn't resist bumping into her shin with the toe of his loafer. At her gasp, he slipped his shoe off and ran his foot down the front of her leg. Her answering squirm brought a smile to his face. Nothing could be more perfect than to have her across the table from him, refusing to talk about what was going on between them but unable to deny the sparks that would never go away.

"Is everything all right?" his mother asked, frowning at Carla.

"Uh-huh. It's fine." She shot him another scathing glance. One his mother didn't miss.

She clicked her tongue. "Leo, you aren't bothering Carla, are you?"

"Would I do something like that?" He planned to bother her, over and over, as soon as he got her back home that night. He was still aggravated at her refusal to let him out their relationship to the rest of his family, but it didn't stop him from wanting to be with her. If she needed more time, she could have it. He'd never go back on his word, so he wouldn't speak to anyone about it, except Alice, who'd already figured out the truth. And Sophie, who would have guessed eventually anyway and wouldn't say a word to anyone else. He'd be a good boy and keep silent even when it tightened his gut into a knot to do so. He'd do it for Carla, because she was worth it. But eventually, the truth would come out. She was fooling herself if she thought they could hide it forever. The women in his family all seemed to have a sixth sense about that sort of thing. Whenever he was serious about a woman, which hadn't happened often in his life, they all zeroed in on the emotion and made the poor woman's life a living hell. With the others, he really hadn't cared as much as he should have. Hadn't protected them from his family's prying ways. But with Carla, everything had changed. If she didn't want anyone to know, fine. He didn't have to like it, but he wouldn't go blabbing about their involvement, either.

And it wasn't just about sex, though that was definitely a driving force in the equation, at least for the moment. The edge for that would fade a little in time, but there were stronger forces at work. He wanted to spend time with her. Get to know her even better than he did now. Take her places and show her off, buy her expensive gifts.

Slow down. Way, way down. Look at what happened with Sophie and Mack.

Yeah. He couldn't let himself forget that. He cared about Carla. A lot. He loved her, though he couldn't admit the truth to her so early in their relationship. He couldn't rush into anything. No one knew what the future might hold, and he didn't want to take unnecessary chances with his heart. If marriage wasn't in the cards for him, fine. Even given the way he felt about Carla, rushing things between them would only end in a lot of heartache if things went wrong.

But if he took it slowly, let her feelings for him develop, they could both be very happy for a *very* long time. The idea held a lot of appeal.

He ran his toes down her leg again and a small squeak erupted from her lips. She flashed him an icy glare. One he returned with a brilliant smile. This was going to be the most interesting meal he'd had in a long time.

Go ahead and pretend we mean nothing to each other, honey. That's not going to last.

He forgot about the noise of his large family, all about Carla's wishes to keep their relationship secret. And it was a relationship. She could call it a fling all she wanted, but he knew the truth. She'd have to face it sooner or later, as he had. They didn't just get together for sex. It had never been that way between them. He stayed the night at her apartment, or she stayed the night at his. He called her cell on his lunch break, just to say hello. She cooked him dinner, and they'd spent a few nights curled up on the couch watching movies. Yeah, most nights ended in the bedroom, but there was so much more to what they had than that. He actually had fun with her. Fun that didn't involve getting between the sheets. He'd never been happier.

But how did she feel about him, really? She felt more than just sexual attraction, but would she ever get brave enough to admit it? He didn't know, but someday soon he intended to find out. And he wasn't going to confess his feelings or emotions until he had a definite answer about hers. He wouldn't open himself up to that kind of hurt. Not ever. Once she was ready to admit how she felt about him, he'd do the same for her. Until then, he'd be better off keeping his feelings to himself.

He tried to rub her leg again, but her foot shot out and smacked into his shin. He grunted in pain and pulled back. For such a little thing, she was certainly strong. Her strength combined with the pointy-toed shoes she wore would leave a bruise come morning. Unfortunately, all eyes turned to him after his surprised reaction, and the din of everyone talking and laughing subsided.

"Leo? What is the matter with you tonight?" His mother shook her head, an exasperated expression on her face. "Stop fooling around and pass me the mashed potatoes."

He passed the stoneware bowl to her before frowning at Carla. She just smiled and went back to eating her roast.

Alice, sitting on his right, gave his shoulder a pinch. He rubbed the sore spot and shot her a dirty look. "What's your problem?"

She smiled, her expression very much like Carla's too sweet, too innocent grin. "Sorry. Pregnancy hormones. I can't help it."

He groaned. Likely excuse.

* * * * *

The rest of the meal passed without much incident, once he realized Carla would likely bruise him in far worse places than his shin if he didn't leave her alone. She'd rushed out of there so fast that, to his disappointment, Leo didn't think he'd see her again that night, but when he got home a half hour later he found her sitting at his door.

She smiled at him, her expression apologetic. "Hi."

"Hey." He propped his hip against the wall and crossed his arms over his chest. "What are you doing here? I figured after this morning, and then tonight, that you wouldn't want to see me again. I assumed I'd be the one waiting for you, begging to get you to listen to me."

He'd had the speech all worked out in his head, too. But now it looked like he wouldn't need it.

She pushed up from the floor and walked to him, placing her hands on her chest. "I don't know what I want, Leo. At this point, everything is a big ball of confusion. But I don't want to fight with you anymore. I just want to be with you, okay? Can I come inside?"

Did she even have to ask? He leaned in to kiss her gently on her lips. "Yeah. Of course. Did you really think I would turn you down?"

If she had, then she really didn't know him very well at all.

"I wasn't sure. I wasn't very nice to you this morning, and I didn't take into account what you might want. I was too busy thinking of myself." She heaved an exasperated sigh. "This is all such a mess."

He unlocked the door and pushed it open, letting her walk inside before he followed her into the apartment. "How do you figure?"

"It wasn't supposed to be like this."

He bristled at her words, a now-familiar aggravation clenching his gut in knots. Why couldn't she just let go of her ridiculous preconceptions? Her stereotypes were going to ruin what they had before they even had a chance to see their relationship's potential. He loved her, damn it, but if she didn't stop being so stubborn he didn't know if he could take it. She needed to give herself the freedom to be happy, without all the unneeded guilt. "How did you expect it to be? What the hell is it you want from me, Carla? I feel like you're pulling me in so many directions at once that I'm going to snap."

He pushed a hand through his hair and closed his mouth, afraid if he said any more she'd run out of his apartment. And this time not come back. If that happened… No. It wouldn't. He wouldn't let it. He'd do whatever he could to see she didn't feel threatened enough to leave. He pulled her into his arms for a quick, tight hug before he backed away and kissed her again, a soft, brief touch of their lips. He dropped his arms and backed up a step, shaking his head. She was so tense her shoulder muscles were bunched and her hands clenched into fists. But then she seemed to relax and held her hands up in front of her in a gesture of surrender.

"Look, I don't want to argue about this. I'm beat. I just need to sit down." A small smile touched her lips. "We can hash this all out later. For now, why don't we just relax for a while?"

That sounded like the best idea he'd heard in a long time. "Okay. Go get comfortable on the couch, find something to watch on TV. I'll get us something to drink and I'll be in with you in a minute."

She frowned, a puzzled expression on her face. "The couch? Why not the bedroom?"

He sighed. As tempting as it sounded, it would only reinforce her notion that there could be nothing but sex between them. That was what she wanted—he saw it in her eyes. Though she said she didn't want to fight anymore, part of her must still feel the need to prove him wrong. Well, he wasn't going to let her do that to him. To them. And for some reason, jumping into bed with her at that particular moment didn't interest him. There would be plenty of time for that later. Now, he wanted to get to know her better, and let her get to know him. To let her get more comfortable being around him, talking to him. Maybe she'd open up to him a little more on the emotional front if he opened up to her first. "I'm not going to take you to bed. Not tonight. Right now, we're going to talk."

"Talk?"

"Yeah, talk. You know, open your mouth and form words."

"Ha, ha. Very funny. I just don't get why you feel the need to spend time talking right now. Aren't there more interesting things for us to be doing?"

Her expression was half seductive, half pleading, and he almost gave in. But he didn't. They both needed emotional comfort much more than physical tonight. How could he explain it to her without scaring her away? "Because we both need it right now. Talking will be good for you. And for us. Trust me on this one, Carla. Go sit down. I'll be right there."

Her frown deepened, but she went into the living room and flopped down on the couch. He went into the kitchen and grabbed a couple cans of soda. With any luck, they'd move past the day's difficulties and come out stronger for it in the end. But first he had to show her again that they got along as well outside the bedroom as they did in it. He thought they'd managed that earlier in the week, but apparently the time they'd spent together hadn't been enough. Tonight would have to be a hands-off night, though the idea really didn't hold a hell of a lot of appeal. With the way she looked in the soft tank top and shorts she'd changed into after the dinner from hell, it was already shaping up to be a very difficult task.

* * * * *

Carla cuddled up next to Leo on the couch, glad that some of the earlier tension seemed to have drained out of the evening. If she forced herself to admit it, she really enjoyed the time they'd spent together, just being close to each other and chatting about so many things she couldn't remember them all now.

He kissed the top of her head, his gaze glued to the action flick on his wide-screen TV. His hand found hers, his fingers squeezing gently. Nothing had ever felt more perfect to her. They'd watched a movie or two together before, always in such easy silence. But the ease itself made unease churn in her gut. She was getting attached. She should have stayed home tonight, gone to bed instead of waiting for him to return from dinner and practically barging into his apartment when he got home. But she hadn't listened to the reason of her conscience, and she ended up falling in love with him a little more for it.

It wasn't just the chemistry between them, though she enjoyed the physical side of their relationship. Very much. Now she wanted more. More for herself, more than Leo would be ready to give for too many years to come. He was just out of college. Still young and technically single since they'd never made any kind of formal commitment to each other. It looked like things were headed that way, but she really couldn't be sure. He'd never come right out and said it to her. He couldn't possibly be thinking of settling down. The way he'd reacted to his sister's impending divorce just proved it to her all the more. Still, she couldn't stop herself from asking questions she really didn't want answers to.

She glanced up and tapped him on the shoulder. "Leo?"

"Hmm?" He looked down at her, his eyes dark beneath his black wire-framed glasses.

"Do you plan on getting married someday?"

As she predicted, his body stiffened and his eyes widened. His throat worked as he swallowed hard, and she swore if she concentrated really hard she'd be able to hear his heart trying to thump right out of his chest. The reaction would have been comical, had the subject not been such a serious one so dear to her heart.

He licked his lips, his gaze darting around the room. Probably looking for the nearest escape route. "Um, I don't know. Maybe. Why do you ask?"

"I was just thinking about Sophie and Mack. It's got to be hard on your sister, going through what she is, trying to hold down a full-time job and raise the kids at the same time."

Leo relaxed, slumping back against the couch cushions. Apparently, talk of marriage only gave him panic attacks when the marriage in question was his own future one. "Yeah. It's too bad. Such a huge shock too, you know? Hearing her news really made me think. I mean, if the two of them can't make it, why would I believe anyone else would?"

Because the world is full of people who can make a decent marriage work. "What about Alice and Jimmy? Lauren and George? Your parents, even? Heck, they've got about the happiest marriage I've ever seen."

"I know. I know. But Sophie and Mack have been together forever. She's never loved anyone else. It just seemed like a once in a lifetime thing to me. And now... He had an affair. Didn't think she was enough to satisfy him."

"They were so young when they got married. They didn't really know what they wanted yet." *Like you really have no idea what you want. You might think you know, Leo, but you don't. It'll take a lot more than twenty-five years to figure it out.*

"What's that supposed to mean?" He let her hand go and pushed back, settling in the corner of the couch with one leg pulled up in front of him. Though he'd only moved a few feet away, it suddenly felt like a mile separated them. "Are you trying to suggest that, because of my age, I don't know what I want?"

"Of course not." *Hell, yes. It's what I've been trying to tell you all along.* "Just that maybe Mack didn't. Sophie may have been ready for marriage at nineteen, but Mack...he probably wasn't. Men take longer to figure out that kind of thing than women do. They mature slower all around. That's all."

"Not necessarily true." His gaze darkened to black and his jaw tensed. His expression grew stormy.

Uh-oh. "I'm just trying to point out what you've already said. You're uncertain, don't know if you even want to get married. Right?"

He frowned. "What's with the sudden talk of marriage, Carla?"

"It's something I've had on my mind a lot lately." *Like since you've been in middle school. Because I was an adult then, and I had dreams of marrying some Prince Charming who would walk in and sweep me off my feet.* She pushed aside the thought, pushed aside all thoughts of commitment and marriage. It obviously made Leo very uncomfortable. Though she knew it would eventually end between them, she didn't want it to end tonight. Not for a little while, at least. She wanted to hang on to Leo for as long as she could before she had to let him go.

"Have you, now?" A small smile flitted across his worried face, a little of the attention fading from his features. "Why is that?"

"In case you hadn't noticed, I'm not as young as you are. Add that to the problem of women only being able to bear children for so long, and you might understand my problem. I want a family someday. Someday soon. I don't want to be considered a senior citizen when my children graduate from high school. I don't want to wait until it's too late, and then regret for the rest of my life not having children."

He licked his lips, his short burst of laughter a little shaky. "Come on, Carla. It's not like you're pushing fifty or anything. And as far as the children go, there are other ways to do that, ways that don't involve marriage."

In other words, as much as you try to protest, you're really not interested. She sighed. So much for them having so much in common. "Yeah, I know. But I don't want to do it alone. I want a family."

Without warning, Leo leaned toward her and kissed her hard on the lips.

She blinked when he pulled back. "What are you doing?"

"I want you, Carla."

"Oh, please. Earlier you said you weren't interested in getting me into bed tonight."

"I changed my mind."

She nearly laughed. He was just trying to distract her from her purpose — which was fine with her. She also wanted to end the conversation before they got into deeper, more uncomfortable territory. Before he asked her to leave, and never come back. She wrapped her arms around his neck and pulled him closer for a kiss.

Chapter Eleven

ଚୈ

Carla sipped her drink and stole a glance at Leo out of the corner of her eye. The music in the bar beat a fast, loud tempo and the dim lights accentuated the dark, cut lines of his features. God, the man was beautiful. The stubble lining his jaw only made him look more rugged, sexier, and seeing him in casual clothes made her stomach flutter just as much as it did when she saw him in the clothes he wore to work.

They'd been seeing each other for nearly two months, and every once in a while she still looked at him and questioned his sanity. What did he see in her? Why did he seem intent on sticking around, taking her out to dinner or the movies, and buying her presents? Why did he seem to enjoy the late night talks about everything from stressful workdays to what the future might hold? One word answered every single one of her questions.

Luck. The stars must have been aligned just perfectly on the night they got together—no any other explanation fit for why a sexy young guy like Leo would waste his time hanging around with her. She nearly snorted. Maybe she should play her lottery numbers while her luck still held. It killed her to think it, but her luck wouldn't hold forever. Not when it came to keeping Leo around—and keeping him interested. Sure, now her life seemed perfect, but what would happen a few months, or a year down the road when a better prospect came along, beckoning to him? And it would. Sooner or later. She harbored no illusions about that.

He gave her that goofy smile she'd seen so many times over the years, but it had changed. A frisson of raw sensuality flashed in his eyes, echoing somewhere deep inside her. She wanted to burn that look into her memory so that she never forgot what she'd been lucky enough to have once in her life. When she was married to a boring man who had no spark, no passion, she would be able to look back on this one perfect moment in time, when she had everything she'd ever wanted within her grasp. The moments before it slid through her fingers like sand at the beach and was washed away by the surf. She sighed, returned his smile with a small, sad one of her own.

She loved him.

How had she let herself be stupid enough to fall for a man she couldn't keep? What had happened to settling down with a nice, stable, older man and raising a family? Leo was supposed to be a fling, an affair, a chance to have a good time with a great guy before she started seriously looking for The One. But now the truth that had been creeping up on her for the past four weeks slammed into her chest with the force of a truck. Leo *was* The One. And she had no hope of keeping him. None.

Pathetic, Carla.

"You okay tonight?" he asked, a frown marring his perfect features. "You seem quiet."

Funny, but she'd been about to ask him the same question. All night he'd been acting strange, like he wanted to say something but lost his nerve every time he opened his mouth. The silences that stretched between them tonight were longer, more uncomfortable than they'd been in the past weeks. His hands shook when he touched her, and whenever they made eye contact his gaze slid away. None of that boded well for their future. Their days together would soon be coming to an end.

"I'm fine." She struggled to put a smile on her face, though his behavior had her heart breaking every time she looked at him. He planned to break it off with her. Why else would he be acting so strangely? Had he met someone else? Maybe the novelty of having an older woman had worn off, and he'd come to realize that the future held nothing for them. Whatever his reasons, the end result would be the same. Their path had been set from night one, and though she wasn't nearly ready for it to be over she hadn't expected anything different. Her heart would be devastated, but she wouldn't react like some sniveling teenager, either. No. She'd take it like the mature, older woman she purported herself to be and accept his decision with grace.

In public.

But as soon as she got home, she'd bury herself in her favorite robe and hit the premium ice cream and the oldie movie channel. For three solid days.

"I'm glad you're okay. You had me worried there for a little while." He set his beer bottle on the bar, his hands shaking so hard he knocked it over. Beer frothed from the open end of the bottle and he batted at it with his napkin. A few choice curses escaped his lips and his face reddened.

Uh-oh. Leo had to be the calmest, most even-tempered person she knew, so if he couldn't stop his hands from shaking it signaled big trouble. *Huge.*

Maybe she should beat him to it and dump *him*. Put him out of the misery he was so obviously in. Then she could go home, have her grieving time, and get back to the real life she'd been living before she took an extended vacation from sanity. She'd opened her mouth to speak, to tell him how she felt, when a tall, leggy blonde wearing a red napkin she apparently thought passed for a dress sidled up next to Leo.

"Wow, Leo, you look great! I haven't seen you in forever." The hussy wrapped her arms around him and gave him a big kiss. Right on the lips.

Carla fumed, fighting to resist her more juvenile urges—which told her to reach out and yank a lock of the tramp's hair. Her hands clenched into fists and her face flamed. Was this the reason he wanted to break up with her? For this…this child?

As soon as Leo untangled himself from the blonde's limbs, she started to sit in his lap, but he stood and stepped next to Carla. "Miranda, this is Carla. My girlfriend."

So the tramp had a name. Miranda? Humph. She would have expected Muffy or Puffy or something equally ridiculous.

Miranda looked Carla up and down, a deep frown on her face. Then she pouted her enormous red lips—*had* to be collagen—and crossed her wispy arms over her overgrown chest. "*You're* the woman he dumped me for?"

Oh, lovely. She glared at Leo. "I have no idea. When did the two of you break up?"

Muffy…er, Miranda, rolled her eyes skyward and chewed on her lower lip, probably trying to locate the one brain cell she possessed. "Um, I think two months ago.

Maybe a little more. Isn't that right, Leo-baby?" She turned her blue-eyed gaze back to Leo. "So what have you been up to? I miss talking to you."

Leo-baby? Was this nursery school or something?

She started for him again and again, and Leo blocked every attempt. "Miranda, this isn't a very good time."

Leo tried to push her away, but she was surprisingly tenacious for someone who couldn't weigh more than a hundred pounds soaking wet.

Soaking? Now *there* was an idea. She could just lure her to the nearest body of water and push her in.

Although, with all the air in her head, she'd probably float.

Shocked at the catty direction of her thoughts, Carla stood up from the stool. She had to get out of there before she considered banging Puffy's head against the bar. She scowled. Too late. Already considered. Time to leave before she gave in to the impulse. "I'll leave you two alone now. You've got some catching up to do."

She rushed to the door and burst out into the cool night, ignoring Leo's call as the door banged shut behind her. That incessant pain-in-the-rear of a voice in her head reminded her—a little too late—that he'd introduced Carla as his girlfriend.

"Shut up!" she growled at the voice, walking out into the parking lot to find her own way home. She should have ended their farce of a relationship before she'd gotten so attached. It had been doomed from the start to end in heartache—though it would have been nice if the heartache and doom had been a little less public.

Once the anger started to ebb, raw pain took its place. She wrapped her arms around herself to ward off the chill, both from the environment and deep within her. She'd avoided spending much time with his friends to avoid a scene just like the one that had happened. Leo, facing his perfect ex-girlfriend—though the perfection was no doubt surgically enhanced—with Carla left to watch in the background as he went off with the woman better suited to him in every way.

But he hadn't gone with Muffy. He stayed with you.

She shook her head, tears threatening to spill from her eyes. The words were little comfort now. She'd walked out, just about given him permission to do whatever he wanted with the younger woman. What kind of fool wouldn't take complete advantage of the situation? She shuddered, wrapped her arms tighter around her middle.

You're such an idiot. All the time you've been waiting for him to act like a kid, but you're the one who did it. The one who ruined everything by channeling your inner teenager.

"Carla! Wait up," Leo called from somewhere behind her. She stopped walking but didn't bother to turn around. If she looked at him, she'd have to admit to herself that she'd overreacted. But, overreactions or not, her choice remained the same. She couldn't stick around just to have him leave months down the road. He might be more mature than she'd first judged him to be, but he couldn't possibly be ready for the lifelong commitment she was looking for.

He caught up with her and grabbed her arm, swinging her around to face him. He sounded slightly breathless, his face flushed. From running out to get her, or something else? His hand came up to cup her cheek and she leaned into the warmth. "I'm sorry about that in there. She's a little...clingy."

Clingy? If she'd been stuck to him any tighter he would have needed surgery to remove her. Well, at least *Buffy* knew a great plastic surgeon. Carla opened her mouth, but snapped it shut right away since she couldn't think of anything to say that wouldn't sound catty. She had to remember her dignity. At this point, it was all she had left.

Dignity? You've got to be kidding me. You're an idiot for even considering letting the man walk out of your life.

"I broke up with her before we started dating," he continued. "I didn't dump her for you, no matter what she said. She's not really my type anyway. She was just someone to pass the time."

Carla shook her head. The more he explained himself, the worse she'd feel about ending it. She needed to sever all ties now, while she still had the capacity to do so. "Could you just take me home, please?"

Why had she ever thought sleeping with Leo—falling in love with him—would be a good idea? His family had been a surrogate family to her for years. Now she wouldn't be able to enjoy another Spencer family dinner, or the traditional party at Christmas. She'd be all alone on Thanksgiving, with nothing but a TV dinner and a frozen pumpkin pie. A teary sigh escaped her lips. She'd be all alone tonight. And every other night for a very, very long time.

"I'll take you home, if that's what you really want. But first I want to talk to you. I would have explained everything if you hadn't stormed out of there like some child."

Child? Bad choice of words. "Excuse me, Mr. Twenty-Five-Year-Old-Super-Stud, if anyone around here deserves to be called a child, it isn't *me*." Even as she said the words, guilt threatened to choke her, but she couldn't take them back. She *wouldn't*. Her mother had always accused her of sabotaging her own happiness, and for the first time in recent memory she had to admit the truth in her mother's words.

Leo snorted. "Could've fooled me."

"Look, I don't want to fight anymore. I just want to go home. If you want to go back inside with what's-her-name, I can always call a cab."

He grabbed her arm when she would have walked away. "Are you out of your mind? Do you think I'm the kind of guy who'd let his woman go home in a cab, alone?"

"Oh, I am *so* not your woman. I'm not *anyone's* woman but my own."

He frowned, his eyes darkening to black under the muted glow of the parking lot lights. With his jaw set in a firm, hard line and his mouth unsmiling, he looked very adult and very, *very* angry.

Oops. Bad idea.

Bad Carla.

He shook his head before he turned and stomped in the direction of his car. "Sure," he growled over his shoulder. "Whatever you say. You can be your own woman as soon as I make sure you get out of here safely. Then you can be whatever you goddamn want to be. But I'm seeing you to your door first, whether you like it or not. Get your ass in the car and I'll take you home."

Rather than risk making any more of a spectacle of herself than she already had, she kept her mouth closed and followed him to his car.

They didn't speak a word to each other on the way home. The tense silence stretched until it opened like a chasm between them, gaping and yawning, ready to suck her into the void. He stole a couple of quick, hard glances at her throughout the ride, which only served to tighten her stomach into a painful knot. She'd never seen him so serious, so angry. She didn't like it one bit. Where was the playful Leo she'd known forever?

Gone. She'd ruined it all when she'd pounded on his door and practically demanded he take her to bed.

He pulled the car into the apartment parking lot, switched off the ignition, and got out and slammed the door. She followed, her hands shaking and her lower lip trembling. A tear slipped down her cheek, but she brushed it away. Now wasn't the time for tears. It was the time for being strong. Being mature and admitting defeat. It never would have worked out between them, not in a forever kind of way. She needed to grow up and let it go. Let *him* go.

Leo insisted on making sure she got through her front door, when she'd just have rather run inside without a goodnight—or a goodbye. But, she had to get it over with. Now or never.

She stopped in front of her door and faced him, trying to hold back the tears she could barely keep at bay. The void she'd felt between them in the car had found a new home. In the pit of her stomach. In her heart. How could she be so stupid to let him walk away? But how could she not? It would be very selfish of her to want to keep him around forever. He was twenty-five. Still too young to settle down into a lifetime commitment.

Hearing about Sophie's divorce had only cemented her thinking. Leo needed to live before he settled down.

Carla had lived, and now she was ready for more. But she didn't have time to wait for him to get older, to be ready. It could be years before that happened. She needed to move on with her life and find someone more suitable for what she was looking for. Why couldn't he have been older? Even thirty and it might have worked. But now, she saw no other way out of the mess she never should have gotten involved with in the first place.

Leo brushed a lock of hair off the side of her face, his thumb caressing her cheekbone as he pulled his hand away. "I'm guessing from your attitude that you wouldn't want to let me in for a little while. I have something I want to talk to you about."

"Not tonight." *Not ever.*

"This is important, Carla."

So is my sanity. If I let you in, I won't have any left. "Leo, I don't think this is going to work."

His eyes widened and his jaw dropped. *"What?"*

"I think we need to stop trying to make this relationship into something it's not."

Surprise flashed across his gaze and he ran a hand through his thick hair. "Where did this come from? It was an argument. It isn't like we haven't had them before. It's not something to break up over."

No, it wasn't, but so many other things factored into her decision. "I've been thinking about it for a while, and tonight, seeing you all nervous like I was, I realized it wouldn't work."

"You've been thinking about ending it? Really?" This time he ran both hands through his hair, a pained expression on his face. He sucked in a deep breath and shook his head. "You've got to be kidding me."

She only wished. "I'm serious. We both know we have no future together. It's better to make a clean break now than deal with something extremely painful and messy down the road." Anguish filled his eyes, and her heart constricted. *Please understand, Leo. This is what's best for you. For us.* "You didn't tell Alice about us, did you?"

His expression darkened, grew stormy, and his hands clenched at his sides. "Why would that matter?" he barked out, his words clipped and harsh.

"She doesn't need to know about this little fling."

His jaw tightened and his nostrils flared, his gaze sparking fire. "Why the hell not?"

"It's…it's just not her business."

"She's my sister, and your best friend. Can you honestly say you think she doesn't know? I don't understand how you can be so clueless about this. About *everything*."

Carla shrugged. "Well, *I* certainly haven't told her."

He turned his back on her and paced the hallway for what seemed like an eternity, his shoulders hunched and his hands shoved into the pockets of his jeans. When he stopped in front of her, his expression had turned to ice. It chilled her to the bone. If she never saw a look like that again, she'd be a happy woman. Though after tonight, she'd doubted she'd see anything else on his handsome face whenever they saw each other.

"You want me to leave? *Fine*," he growled. "You want things to be over between us? *Whatever.* I can't hold you to me if you don't want to stay, and I refuse to beg for something you obviously think is a lost cause. But before I go, I'm going to speak my mind and you're going to keep your mouth shut and listen."

He yanked his hands from his pockets, spread them in front of him and glared at her, a hint of sadness in his eyes. "I've never wanted any other woman but you. *Never.* You're in my thoughts, my fantasies, my dreams. All the time. I've been in love with you since I was seven years old. It hasn't faded with time, Carla, it's only grown stronger. A love that lasting doesn't fade away. *Not ever.* I just thought you should know that."

She gaped at his confession, her mind too muddied to form words. Never in the past weeks had he even hinted that his feelings for her ran so strong. Yes, he'd told her he cared about her, but love had never come into the picture. It took her breath away and made tears form behind her lids. She tried to hold them back, but they fell anyway, probably staining her cheeks with rivers of watery mascara since she hadn't thought to wear waterproof. What did he expect her to say to his admission?

Didn't he understand that she was trying to save them both a lot of heartache a few months, or years down the road?

"It's not you, Leo. It's nothing personal. We're just too different, we want different things out of life."

He gave her a tight grin, the agony in his gaze making her want to reach out and hold him. She took a step toward him, but he shook his head. "That's where you're wrong. It's *completely* personal. You don't want me because of who you knew me as when I was a kid. I'm not a kid anymore, and I thought I could show you that. I thought if I tried hard enough, you'd see me for the man I've become. You'd give me a chance, finally, to show you how good we are together, and how incredible we would be. I guess I was wrong." He pulled a small box out of his pocket and thrust it into her hand. "I was planning to give you this tonight, but I never got the chance. Keep it. Sell it. Throw it out the window for all I care. I don't give a shit what you do with it. I'll never have any use for it now. *Ever.*"

He stalked down the hall to his door, unlocked it and yanked it open, storming inside and slamming it shut so hard she jumped back a few steps.

Hot tears stung her eyes, sliding down her cheeks in rivulets. She swiped at them to no avail, finally giving in and letting herself sob, right there in the hallway. What had she done?

The knot in her stomach turned into a ball of ice as she stared at the black velvet box clutched in her palm. She should put it away without looking at its contents, but curiosity compelled her to lift the lid. An anguished moan slipped from her lips when she saw the diamond solitaire inside.

Chapter Twelve

ೋ

Heavy, insistent pounding on her front door woke Carla up around three in the morning "Carla! Open up!"

What the heck? She shook off sleep, sat up on the edge of the bed. Was she dreaming?

"Come on, Carla! It's an emergency."

She was halfway through a yawn when two things registered at once—one, Leo was banging on her door, and two, he said "emergency". The remnants of sleep dissolved and she shot out of the bedroom to the front door, throwing it open. He barged in, nearly knocking her over. "Get dressed."

"What? What's the matter?"

"Alice is having the baby. Jimmy's on his way, but he's just driving back from his business trip and doesn't know if he's going to make it on time. She's at the hospital all by herself, and she wants us there pronto."

Anxiety skittered down her spine and she gulped. "I thought she wasn't due for two more weeks?"

"Try telling my future nephew that." He scrubbed a hand down his face—a face that looked as tired and bone-weary as she felt. "Go get dressed so we can get out of here, okay? We don't have time to be fooling around here."

"Okay. Give me two minutes." She left him standing in the entryway, a pained, tense expression on his face and his eyes hooded, as she rushed to the bedroom to pull on some clothes.

She grabbed a pair of jeans and a shirt off the floor—the ones she'd worn earlier on their disastrous final date. The thought gave her pause for a few seconds, but she shook off the uneasiness. Alice needed her. Alice wouldn't care if Carla showed up in a bathrobe and bunny slippers. What did it really matter if she wore wrinkled clothes? And Leo…he was still so angry she doubted if he'd notice much past the fact that he wanted to strangle her. She shoved her feet into a pair of canvas sneakers, grabbed her purse, and rushed out the bedroom door.

She stopped in front of Leo, panting and sweating from exertion and nerves. "I'm all set."

His gaze raced up and down her body before he gave her a terse nod. "Good. Let's go."

Twenty minutes later, they raced into Alice's room. Alice glared when she saw them approach the bed, her eyes narrowing. "Where the *hell* have you two been? I've been waiting forever, no one will give me anything to help with this pain, and I need to crush someone's head!"

Leo took a step back, his eyes wide. His throat worked as he swallowed hard. "We're here now. Just relax. It'll all be over soon." He turned to the nurse who stood by the monitors, looking suspiciously like she was fighting laughter. "It will, right?"

She nodded. "She's just about fully dilated. She'll be pushing very soon." The nurse kept speaking to Leo, but glanced toward Alice and raised her voice. "She would have been able to have an epidural if she hadn't waited so long to come in. By the time she got here, it was too late."

Alice stuck her tongue out at the nurse. "I've been having false labor off and on for two weeks, and I'm not due until the end of the month. How was I supposed to— *ow*!"

Carla rushed over to her bedside and took Alice's hand. "Just calm down, sweetie. It's going to be fine."

Alice's grip tightened on her fingers until it felt like she'd broken every bone in her hand. Carla pried her hand away with a grimace and brushed her friend's damp hair out of her eyes. "Wow. Have you been working out?"

Leo slumped into a chair in the corner, far away from the business end of the bed. He looked decidedly pale, and Carla chuckled to herself. Amazing how big, strong, take-charge kind of guys turned into wusses at the sight of a little childbirth.

"I need drugs." Alice's voice held a deceptively calm tone, one Carla had a feeling would fade as soon as the next contraction hit. "I won't make it through this if I don't get drugs. I'll die, and then my husband will sue the hospital for malpractice."

"Um, Alice, I don't think you want to threaten something like that," Carla warned, but the nurse shook her head.

"Don't worry about it. I've been here for fifteen years. I've heard much worse."

"And I'm sure it's all deserved." Alice narrowed her eyes at the woman. "You people are all sadists. Every one of you. Carla, when you and Leo have children, *don't* have them here."

Carla shot a worried glance toward Leo. He paled even more, but didn't confess their breakup to his sister.

For that, Carla let out a sigh of relief. Alice had enough going on now without *that* revelation.

"I'll take that into consideration."

And then chaos exploded in the room. Alice cried out in pain. Jimmy burst into the room moments later, saving Carla from helping Alice through another contraction. The doctor followed shortly, telling Alice it was time to push. Not wanting to see the actual birth—hey, braveness and an iron stomach only carried a person so far—Carla beckoned to Leo to follow her out of the room.

She walked into a small waiting area at the end of the hall, determined to stick around to make sure both Alice and the baby made it through okay.

"Thanks for coming with me tonight." Leo came up behind her and put his hands on her shoulders. She leaned back against him, her heart rate finally slowing down and the nausea slipping out of her stomach.

"I guess none of this turned out the way anyone had planned."

She shrugged, determined not to let him see how heartbroken she was after their fight. They could discuss their breakup later, if he felt the need. Now she only wanted to think about Alice and the baby. "Alice couldn't help it."

"I'm not talking about Alice, and you know it."

"I know." She ducked out of his grasp and took a seat on one of the chairs that lined the waiting room, her heart thumping in her chest. "I don't really want to talk about this right now. This isn't the right time."

He sat next to her and rested his hand on her thigh. His warmth seeped through her jeans to her skin and made the tears want to start all over again. She sniffled, tried to push him away, but he wouldn't budge.

"Carla?" When she refused to look at him, he tipped her chin up with his finger. "Did you open the box?"

Her jaw dropped and her eyes widened. "Your sister is in there, having your nephew. Why are you being so selfish?"

"I think we have at least a little while to wait." A soft chuckle escaped him. "Did you open the box, Carla?"

"Well...yeah, I did."

A hint of a smile played on his lips. "Did you like it?"

The waterworks started fresh again, and she soon found herself crushed up against Leo's chest, his hand massaging her back. Relief flooded her, relief she hadn't expected. Maybe she hadn't ruined everything. Maybe, even after all she'd said, he still wanted her in his life. And if he did, she wouldn't hesitate. Not even one second.

"Should I take that as a yes?"

"Yes," she mumbled — or tried to. It was hard to speak with her face shoved up against his hard, warm chest.

"We both made mistakes. You in not trusting in us, and me for not confessing my intentions sooner. But we can get past all that. I don't want this to be over." He rested his hand on the back of her head, his fingers stroking through her hair. "I don't want to lose you, not when I've finally got everything I want. Please tell me you want that, too."

If only it were that simple. She pulled away from him and shook her head, glancing up to meet his eyes. "We don't have the same goals."

"Oh, yeah? We've never compared goals to find out. Since we've got a little while to wait, now's a perfect opportunity. I'll start." He threw her a devastating smile that did things to her she was pretty sure had to be illegal in most states. At the same time, it soothed her frayed nerves.

"Okay."

"I want a family, a wife to come home to every night after work. I want a dog, and maybe a cat, and a house in the suburbs in a great neighborhood like the one my parents live in. I want to do things like baseball and PTO. Family vacations and amusement parks, and even late night feedings and changing diapers. Hell, I'll even throw in a minivan if it would make you happy."

She hiccuped and sniffled through her tears. He wanted everything she wanted. Her heart swelled as she looked at him. Could it be possible? Would she really get to keep him forever? "No minivan, Leo." He kissed the top of her head and she laughed.

He let out a long, dramatic sigh. "Good thing, cause I really couldn't see myself driving something like that. I'm more of an SUV kinda guy, really. What about everything else? The home and the family and the vacations?"

She nodded before she could stop herself. His eyes widened before a slow smile spread over his face. And then he pulled the ring box out of his pocket.

She blinked. "How…"

His smile widened, turning sly. "I snagged it off the counter while you were getting dressed."

She opened her mouth to speak, but he shushed her with a kiss. When he broke away — entirely too soon, in her opinion — his expression had grown serious. "Let's see if I can do this right this time. I love you, Carla. I always have. I'd rather spend my life alone than with someone other than you. No silly little age difference is going to change that. Will you marry me?"

If she married him, she'd have a lifetime of happiness with the man she loved. If she worried about their differences, which suddenly didn't seem so vast at all, she'd be miserable for the rest of her days. What choice could she make?

Duh. Her stupid, selfish pride only went so far before her heart took over. "I love you, too, and yes."

"Yes?"

A look of such surprise and hope crossed his face that she couldn't help but laugh. "Yes, Leo. *Yes.*"

He looked like he wanted to say more, but Jimmy rushed into the waiting room then, a huge smile on his face. "Alice had the baby. It's a girl. Six pounds, eleven ounces."

Carla frowned. "A girl?"

"I thought the ultrasound showed Alice was having a boy," Leo said.

Jimmy shrugged. "Just another one of life's little surprises. You never know what you're going to get."

Carla laughed at the sage words. She could definitely relate to that.

* * * * *

Leo and Carla walked hand in hand into Alice's hospital room. His heart swelled at the sight of his sister holding his tiny niece. She was small and wrinkled and pink, with dark hair and Alice's full lips, and just about the cutest thing he'd ever seen. He couldn't wait to see Carla holding *their* children—which would be very soon if he had his way.

She'd hinted around that she didn't want to wait—something about her not getting any younger. Hell, if she wanted to start trying tomorrow, he was game. Whatever she wanted, she could have. Those few hours after he thought he'd lost her had been the worst in his life. He'd paced his apartment, unable to settle down, unable to sleep. Wanting to go to Carla and find a way to shake some sense into her. In the end, the matter had been taken out of his hands. He'd have to find a way to thank Alice and the little one for that later.

"How are you feeling?" he asked Alice, smiling down at the small bundle swaddled in soft-looking pink blankets.

"Great. Tired, but great. Isn't she adorable? Too bad, though, about all the boy clothes I have. I'm going to have to exchange that all this week."

He laughed. "Where's Jimmy?"

"Went to get coffee. He'll be back in a few minutes." She glanced at Carla and smiled. "What is that on your hand?"

Carla blinked. "It's, uh…"

"An engagement ring," Leo supplied, earning a swat in the arm from Carla.

"You don't just drop something like that on someone," she scolded, but he laughed it off. He was too happy to worry about after-childbirth etiquette. And Alice knew what he'd been through to get to this point in his life. Hell, she knew just about everything. She'd understand.

"Oh, please. Give it a rest, Carla." Alice shook her head and smiled. "Who do you think helped him pick out the ring?"

Carla glanced at him, her eyes narrowed. "You told me you didn't tell her."

"He didn't," Alice butted in. "I recognized his handwriting on the card with the flowers he sent you. I put it all together what with you'd told me about your younger man and all the secrecy issues you both seemed to suddenly have. Really, it wasn't that hard to figure out."

"You've known for that long?" Carla asked, narrowing her eyes even more until they looked like tiny slits—which didn't seem very fair considering Alice was the one who should have said something to her, being her best friend and all.

Alice nodded. "Well, I knew about *your* attraction to *him* for that long, anyway. But with him, I knew how he felt about you for a lot longer. Do you want to hear about the time—"

Oh, no. This was *so* not going to happen right now. "Why don't we get going and let the family have a little privacy. My sister is obviously still a little delirious from childbirth." Leo steered Carla toward the door, tossing his sister a wink over his shoulder. "Alice, we'll stop back tomorrow. Enjoy your baby."

"What was that all about?" Carla pinched his shoulder playfully as they walked down the hall toward the building exit. "Is it something I need to know about you before we tie the knot?"

Knowing Alice, her story would cause endless embarrassment on his part, and endless teasing on Carla's.

"We can talk about it later. We have all the time in the world."

Epilogue

❧

"Have I mentioned how tired I am lately?" Carla settled next to Leo on the couch and rested her hand on his knee.

He put his laptop on the coffee table and shifted to face her. A small smile etched her face. He frowned and adjusted his glasses. "What's the matter? Too many hours at work again?"

The smile widened. "Maybe. Think I should cut back a little?"

He didn't even need to think about his answer. In the two months since they'd eloped — the night after his niece Katherine, was born — he'd been bugging her to do just that. He made decent money, and between the two of them they had enough saved, that they could live comfortably with her working part-time. And eventually not working at all, though he doubted that would ever happen. "Yeah, I do."

She let out a sigh laced with relief. "Good. I'm glad you feel that way. I was actually thinking of taking a leave of absence for a while. Think we can swing it?"

He cocked his head to the side. What was her game? Was she trying to tell him she'd found a new job? Or maybe had tired of her career and wanted to try something new? "I know we can. What brought this on?"

She shrugged. Her eyes widened. The picture of innocence. "I just don't think all the chemicals at work would be good for the baby."

His heart lodged in his throat, making speech difficult. His stomach flip-flopped and all his blood rushed in his ears. Had he heard her wrong? Baby? "The *what*? Excuse me? What did you just say?"

"With all the perm and color chemicals floating around in the air, I don't know if that's really a good atmosphere for me and the little guy." She patted her flat stomach, her expression serene. "What do you think?"

"You're pregnant?"

She nodded. "I found out this afternoon. And then I told Nikki that I probably wouldn't be able to work for a while."

Her fingers squeezed his knee, but he barely felt the pressure. His mind was still trying to wrap around the idea that his wife was having a baby. A baby. A real, live child. He'd be a father in less than a year. A smile spread over his face as joy welled inside him. He'd wanted this, but hadn't expected it so soon. Though he should have. They hadn't even bothered being careful since the wedding.

"How far along are you?"

"Ten weeks."

Ten weeks? They'd only been married for eight. "The night Katherine was born. The night you tried to push me out of your life…"

Her tongue darted out to wet her lips. "I didn't know then. I had no idea. I didn't even get suspicious about it until a few weeks ago."

He cupped her chin in his palm and leaned in for a slow, smoldering kiss. He'd never been happier, never felt more love for her than he did at that moment. When he pulled back, he smiled. "I love you, Carla. I told you we were meant to be together. Even if I hadn't convinced you to marry me that night, you never would have been able to kick me out of your life."

Surprisingly, a tear slid down her cheek. "I never wanted you out of my life, Leo. Sometime during the time we dated, I'd come to realize you were exactly what I was looking for. I just didn't think it could work out in the end. I didn't dare hope."

He shook his head. "You should have listened to me. I knew the whole time, even before we started seeing each other. I knew what I wanted. Why didn't you trust that?"

More tears coursed down her cheeks, but she smiled. "I needed to learn it on my own. For so long I saw you as the little kid who used to annoy me. Someone I had nothing in common with. But time changed that, and it took me a little longer to see you as something else."

"But you do now?"

"Yes. I wouldn't have it any other way." She stood up and took his hand, tugging him to his feet. "If we have a girl, I was thinking about the name Abby."

She kissed him hard and fast before she stepped back and smiled. "For a boy, maybe Michael or Andrew."

"Those are good names." He settled his hand on her stomach, still trying to come to grips with the whole thing. How could she be thinking about names so soon? "I guess we're going to have to start house hunting a little sooner than we'd planned."

She blinked up at him. "Can we afford it?"

"If you stop spending your money on shoes we'll be fine."

She laughed. "Why would I need any more shoes? I have a new obsession now."

He hated to even ask. "What would that be?"

"Baby clothes."

Well, damn. He'd better start praying for a boy now. If they had a girl, with any luck she wouldn't inherit her mother's penchant for shopping. Otherwise he'd be broke by the time the child was ten, because he didn't think he'd be able to refuse either of them anything. Ever again.

Enjoy An Excerpt From:

GRAVE SILENCE

Copyright © ELISA ADAMS, 2005.

All Rights Reserved, Cerridwen Press

ॐ

The dreams always ended the same. She didn't remember how they began, or much of what happened in between, but the last bit burned bright in her mind when she woke — the hum of the baseball bat moving through the air, the sickening crack as it connected with human flesh and bone. *Her* flesh. *Her* bones. Pain exploded in her head with every blow. That single moment in time, the horror she relived almost every night, was all she remembered of her former life.

The battered condition of her body led the doctors to believe she had a history of long-term abuse. Her mind, muddied and confused, hadn't been able to confirm or deny their suspicions. The police had found her one night wandering the streets, bruised and bloodied, not even sure of her own name. Alone. Confused. *Forgotten.*

They had bad news for her, they'd said, as well as good news. The bad news was that she couldn't remember. And the good news...

She couldn't remember.

Weeks of surgery and recovery to fix her ruined face had followed. Through it all they'd tried to find the family that had abandoned her, but not even a shred of evidence rewarded their efforts. With no other options, no distant relatives who could come to take her away, they tossed her to the wolves. Being a minor, they made her a ward of the state. Several months after that night, they placed her in her first foster home.

That was when the dreams had begun. Horrible, terrifying things that came in the night when she sat silent on the end of her bed, sleepless, waiting for daylight to come. At first, the baseball bat was all she'd been able to see. She'd felt it, too, the pain she hadn't quite been able to forget. Felt it as a physical blow, tearing her apart from the inside out, though when she woke up her body showed no signs of injury.

After a few weeks the dreams changed, slowly morphed into visions of the future. She saw others, beaten and abused. Abandoned. Dead. One night she saw her foster mother's kind face in her mind, her eyes closed and a trickle of blood leaking from the corner of her mouth.

That was the night her foster father, in a drunken rage, had murdered his wife.

Sitting in a police cruiser sometime in the middle of the night, watching the watery swirls of blue and white lights flashing across the rain-soaked pavement, she remembered something her mind had long begged her to forget.

Her name was Caitie, and she was six years old.

* * * * *

Her stomach churned as she walked the few blocks from her hotel to the police station. Cold sweat peppered her brow. She swiped at it with her palm. *Cool it. They can't do anything to you that hasn't been done before.* The stares, the doubts, the snickers behind her back. An occupational hazard, of a sort. She'd been called a fraud, a charlatan, and many things worse. A few times, a murderer. She expected it, but being treated like some kind of circus sideshow took its toll.

Her hands shook by the time she reached the door of the small brick building housing the Longford PD. *God, Caitlin, what are you doing here?*

This visit wasn't usual—if she could claim to have a usual, in her line of work. This time, the police department hadn't contacted her. *She'd* contacted *them.*

Would they accept what she had to say? The detective she'd spoken to on the telephone had invited her to come in and talk more about her theories. What would he think when she explained what she'd seen?

Had she seen anything at all?

She laughed. Maybe one too many unsolved murders and missing persons cases had finally cracked her sanity. She couldn't go into this riddled with self-doubt. They would know, and they'd laugh her right out of town.

The beep of a car horn somewhere in the distance spurred her into action. *Sink or swim, Caitlin. Just do it, already.* She pulled open the door and stepped inside.

A blast of icy air hit her, a window air conditioning unit whirring in the stillness of the small, square room. A wooden bench and a couple of chairs sat in a small alcove near the front door. Several desks littered the room in the haphazard fashion she'd seen once or twice in very small police departments. She smiled. Organized chaos at its finest. She glanced down the short hallway to the right, saw nothing but closed doors.

The lone occupant of the room, a dark-haired man with an even darker—yet somehow intriguing—expression, snagged her attention. He sat behind a desk in the far corner of the room, telephone receiver to his ear, his feet propped on the metal surface of the cluttered desk with his legs crossed at the ankles. He looked to be in his late thirties, maybe early forties, handsome in a brooding way. But it wasn't his looks, necessarily, that had caught her attention. There was something about him, intangible but strong, that made her unable to look away. Charisma, maybe. Good, old-fashioned sex appeal. Whatever it was, it certainly was potent. Familiar, even. But that was crazy. She'd never met the man before. She would have remembered someone like him.

His tie hung loose around his neck, the top buttons of his charcoal gray shirt undone to reveal a white undershirt over tanned skin. Her breath stuck in her lungs and her eyes lingered there, at that spot. Did the men in Longford all look this good, or was she just lucky to run into one of the finer specimens on her first day in town?

Cut it out. You're acting like you've never seen a man before. And haven't you learned not to go fishing for dates in police stations?

Oh yeah. She'd most definitely learned *that* lesson.

He glanced up, his gaze locking with hers in a way that nearly sucked the breath from her lungs. His smile didn't quite reach his weary eyes, faded to a frown after only a second. He hung up the phone.

"What can I do for you?" His deep, husky voice rumbled through her, his deep, smooth tone quickening her pulse.

"I'm Caitlin McKay. I'm here to see Detective Harris." Her mouth twitched in a nervous smile. She dug her fingernails into her palms as anxiety rose in her stomach, threatened to overwhelm her.

"Now why did I know you were going to say that?" He narrowed his gray eyes and sat up in the chair. His intense gaze raked her body, from head to toe and back again, maybe more an intimidation tactic than an interested perusal.

A lump formed in her throat and she revised her original assessment. Handsome, yes. Definitely brooding. Dark. Dangerous. But not familiar at all. Foreign, and downright scary. A man who could be a serious detriment to a woman's well-being. A warning shot through her. *Stay away from this one. He'll only bring you trouble.* "Is there a problem?"

He raised an eyebrow, shrugged a shoulder. "You're definitely not what I expected."

"I'm so sorry if I've disappointed you."

If her sarcastic tone affected him, he didn't show it. Stoic and unsmiling, he pushed himself out of his chair and walked over to her. "Whether or not you disappoint me remains to be seen. I'm Detective Harris. Why don't we get this over with so I can get back to my job?"

"By all means. I wouldn't want to disrupt your social hour." She gestured toward the phone on his desk.

He fixed her again with that slate gray, cold as granite stare and pushed up from his seat. Her legs threatened to quake, her face heated, but she bit back a derisive reply. She waited, as calm and collected as her rioting senses would allow, for him to break eye contact first. He blinked, shook his head, and walked away down the hall.

She rolled her eyes. She'd met men like him before. The true Alpha. The lone wolf. Leader of the pack. Good thing she didn't abide by pack law. "Do you expect me to follow you?"

"That would be preferable, Miss McKay, unless you think we can conduct this interview telepathically." He didn't even look back, opened the door at the end of the hall and disappeared inside.

Of all the nerve.

Available
from
Ellora's Cave

In Moonlight
Elisa Adams, Liddy Midnight, J.C. Wilder

Full Moon Magic By J.C. Wilder

Esme Proctor is the seventh daughter of a seventh daughter in a legendary lineage of witches. Betrothed at a young age, she is whisked off to live in near solitude until the morning of her marriage. Desperate to escape her upcoming nuptials, she conjures a lover to take her virginity and free her from the betrothal contract.

Only things don't work out quite as she expected…

Half Moon Magick By Liddy Midnight

The mage Black Isolde has long had visions of a gorgeous, sexy man. When he appears in the flesh, she can't be certain whether he's the man of her dreams or a nightmare of the worst kind: a Dark Mage.

Harmon has devoted his life to the destruction of Dark Mages. His work has required him to walk a knife-edge between darkness and light. Isolde's purity balances the shadows he's acquired, but he may have spent too long in the darkness to ever be free of its taint.

Wishful Thinking By Elisa Adams

In need of a change of scenery, workaholic Jack Cullen takes a vacation to an isolated island in northern New England. He isn't prepared for the unusual antics of the inn's owner, a woman claiming to be a witch, or his powerful attraction to her mysterious niece.

Mia just wants to live her life in peace. Raising her daughter by herself coupled with her job as a healer, she doesn't have much time to pursue a relationship. Since Jack is only around for a few weeks, he seems like the perfect solution to her loneliness—until the time comes for him to leave, and she finds herself wishing he'd stay.

Enjoy Excerpts From:
In Moonlight

FULL MOON MAGIC

Esmerelda Proctor stared at the wedding gown in absolute horror. The white silk and tulle creation was nestled in a bed of ivory tissue paper in an oversized cardboard box closely resembling a coffin. The bodice and long, fitted sleeves were covered in delicate seed pearls, glittering crystals and yards of Brussels lace. The voluminous tulle skirt was barely restrained by the yards of tissue paper wrapped around it. At the bottom of the box, her mother's wedding tiara was nestled in its own bed of tissue paper next to dainty silk slippers.

Her eyes slid shut and a feeling of impending disaster washed over her. Maybe it was a mistake and she'd imagined the gown on her bed. A half-laugh, half-sob escaped and her hands fisted. She took a deep breath and slowly released it before allowing herself to open her eyes.

The gown was still there.

"Drat."

Fashioned for her great-great grandmother, the original Esmerelda, the gown was fit for a princess and, despite its age, was as pristine as the day it was first worn. Her great-grandmother, Angelina, had worn the dress, as had her grandmother, Brianna, and finally her mother, Carolan. It was part and parcel of being the seventh Proctor daughter of a seventh Proctor daughter legacy.

She, Esmerelda Julianna Proctor, was the last of her line and destined to wear this dress.

Only she'd been hoping it wouldn't be this soon. Her lips twisted. Not to mention the fact that the dress would never fit her without magical assistance. Carolan had been a sleek size eight, while Esme was a sturdy size sixteen. She sighed again, poked at a sleeve and felt something stiff tucked into the edge of the box.

A thick, cream linen envelope peeked out from the layers of cloth and paper. She picked it up and her stomach plummeted. The paper was obviously expensive and on the back was her father's seal, a raven with a dagger clutched in its claws.

She broke the scarlet wax with a fingernail, tipped the envelope over and a cassette tape fell out. Her hand trembled as she picked it up and hurried to her stereo to shove it into the player. She pushed the play button.

"Esmerelda." Her father's voice sounded from the speakers. "The day has come for you to fulfill your duties to your family and marry the Montgomery heir as was set forth in the betrothal contract. By now you've received the wedding gown and everything you'll need for the ceremony. The car will pick you up Saturday morning at 10:00 a.m. and the ceremony is set for 10:45 a.m. sharp. If anything is missing or does not fit properly, have Shani contact my assistant and they will take care of the issue." There was a slight pause and the sound of a heavily indrawn breath.

"Do not disappoint me."

The tape whirred, then fell silent. Esme stared at the player in total disbelief.

"This can't be happening." She crumpled the envelope in her hand and her stomach cramped with betrayal. The message hadn't contained even the slightest hint of affection that a father should have shown his daughter. Instead, it had been a cold and impersonal message, as if he were speaking to a complete stranger.

Her lip curled. Edward Barrows-Proctor hadn't even granted her permission to contact him. Instead she'd been directed to go through her guard, who in turn would contact her father's assistant. She bit her lip hard to prevent the sob that threatened to erupt.

My father doesn't give a damn about me.

HALF MOON MAGICK

Black Isolde carefully poured a small amount of oil over the water in her wide bowl of hammered copper . The scents of lavender and mint rose as the water warmed the oils. She inhaled deeply, closing her eyes for a moment, letting the fragrances relax her body and clear her mind. She opened her eyes and stared into the bowl, her gaze unfocused.

The surface of the oil smoothed, the shimmer of the pouring subsiding. The image of the cottage ceiling appeared briefly. In its place came swirls of color, blues and greens, random shapes that gradually resolved into recognizable figures. Tree boughs heavy with summer leaves grew to fill the vision, her perspective falling lower until only the huge trunks loomed around her.

The forest she saw was unknown to her, a quiet place of deep shadows. 'Twas too quiet. Unsettled, she searched the vision for other signs of life, birds in flight or squirrels at play. Nothing moved in the dappled light.

Mist began to rise from the ground, wreathing the trees in first gray and then white as it gathered and thickened. Through the gauzy streamers came a man.

Oh, dear Goddess, what a man!

She'd seen him before, in dreams of prophecy and visions of her future. Now he strode boldly toward her, parting the mist. Behind and around him crowded the denizens of the forest. Flocks of birds and families of animals — deer and wolves, bears and rabbits — soared and romped as the fog dispersed.

Above him, sparrows flew around a hawk, unconcerned, indeed teasing the raptor with close dives. The sly tap of a wingtip sent them tumbling downward in a feathery cascade. Isolde could almost hear their excited chatter as they recovered and climbed to begin their game anew.

Like the creatures he led, the man wore nothing more than the Goddess had blessed him with.

Had She ever blessed him!

WISHFUL THINKING

Copyright © ELISA ADAMS, 2004.

Clara sighed. The young. They never understood anything. "Many spells are performed at night, Mia. You, of all people, should know that."

"Oh, believe me, I understand. What I don't get is all the secrecy. You only sneak around behind everyone's back if you've got some idea cooked up, or if there's something seriously wrong." Mia frowned, her expression darkening. "Please tell me there isn't something seriously wrong with you, or Uncle Lou."

"Oh for Goddess' sake, I'm fine. I was making a wish. That's all."

"A wish." Mia repeated, not looking at all sure that she believed it.

Clara nodded as she picked up her crutches and made her way to the gazebo steps. "It seems to be the only way I'm going to get what I want." She ignored Mia's silent offer of help and hobbled down the steps, leaning on the metal crutches for support. She was halfway across the yard before Mia followed her.

"Slow down before you fall and do some more damage to yourself," she said, stopping on the stone path in front of her so Clara had to come to a halt or knock her niece over.

"I'm sixty-four, not a hundred and four. I'm perfectly aware of what my limitations are," Clara told her, ignoring Mia's pointed gaze at the cast on her leg. "You need to worry about yourself and stop trying to mother everyone else. Especially those of us who are older than you."

Mia wasn't deterred that easily, no matter how much Clara had hoped she'd be.

"What is it that you could possibly want? You've got everything you need right here." Mia sighed heavily and shook her head. Clara felt the annoyance radiating from her niece and felt guilty for causing it. But, in the end, it would be worth it.

"It's nothing you need to worry about, Mia. Honestly, you're much too serious for someone so young. Live a little."

She just wanted Mia to be happy. The girl had been alone for too long. She deserved a home and a father for Frances. She had such a nurturing, caring manner, and Clara hated to see it wasted on an aging couple and a tiny bed and breakfast when she could put it to much better use.

Mia *said* she was happy here, but Clara wondered. There had to be some small part of her itching to leave, to live her life the way she was meant to. The girl was only twenty-eight. If her life kept going along its current path, she'd stay single and alone, and never leave Bennett Island.

Mia argued that she had Frances, and yes, Clara understood that the child took a lot of her time. But Frances was happy and healthy, if not a little bit mischievous, and everyone doted on her for the summers they spent on the Island. Mia had no one to make her feel special. Everyone needed someone like that in their lives, and Mia had been without for too long—three years last month. Her grieving was over, and it was time for her to move on. But, for some reason, the girl seemed insistent on moving in permanently and hiding away from the rest of the world.

Clara wasn't about to sit back and let *that* happen. Mia needed a gentle nudge—which Clara was all too happy to provide. She gave her niece a big smile and gestured to the waning moon above. "There will be a new moon soon."

"I'm aware of that," Mia answered, her tone laced with suspicion.

"That's the perfect time for self-improvement."

Mia laughed at that, which Clara took as a good sign. "Are you planning to get a makeover?"

"No, dear. But it would be a good time for *you* to embark on something new—like a relationship."

Mia let out groan and turned away, hurrying the final few steps to the back door. "I'll be inside if you need me. Please be careful out here."

"Goodnight, Mia." Clara laughed to herself as she watched Mia walk away. The girl was nothing if not predictable. Just the mention of new relationships had her running in the other direction. She didn't understand, despite all that had happened in her young life, that she couldn't fight her destiny. And Clara knew Mia's destiny did *not* lie on this little island—at least not in the way she thought it did.

That was how Clara had come to this—her last resort, a wish spell in the middle of the night. With any luck, the spell would take quickly and bring some happiness for Mia to the island soon. The tourist season was winding to a close, winter was fast approaching, and in a little less than a month Clara's Bed and Breakfast would shut its doors until spring. This might be Clara's chance for several months to help Mia find some true happiness. Clara chuckled to herself.

Sometimes fate needed a little push.

Why an electronic book?

We live in the Information Age — an exciting time in the history of human civilization, in which technology rules supreme and continues to progress in leaps and bounds every minute of every day. For a multitude of reasons, more and more avid literary fans are opting to purchase e-books instead of paper books. The question from those not yet initiated into the world of electronic reading is simply: *Why?*

1. ***Price.*** An electronic title at Ellora's Cave Publishing and Cerridwen Press runs anywhere from 40% to 75% less than the cover price of the exact same title in paperback format. Why? Basic mathematics and cost. It is less expensive to publish an e-book (no paper and printing, no warehousing and shipping) than it is to publish a paperback, so the savings are passed along to the consumer.

2. ***Space.*** Running out of room in your house for your books? That is one worry you will never have with electronic books. For a low one-time cost, you can purchase a handheld device specifically designed for e-reading. Many e-readers have large, convenient screens for viewing. Better yet, hundreds of titles can be stored within your new library — on a single microchip. There are a variety of e-readers from different manufacturers. You can also read e-books on your PC or laptop computer. (Please note that Ellora's

Cave does not endorse any specific brands. You can check our websites at www.ellorascave.com or www.cerridwenpress.com for information we make available to new consumers.)

3. *Mobility.* Because your new e-library consists of only a microchip within a small, easily transportable e-reader, your entire cache of books can be taken with you wherever you go.

4. *Personal Viewing Preferences.* Are the words you are currently reading too small? Too large? Too... ANNOYING? Paperback books cannot be modified according to personal preferences, but e-books can.

5. *Instant Gratification.* Is it the middle of the night and all the bookstores near you are closed? Are you tired of waiting days, sometimes weeks, for bookstores to ship the novels you bought? Ellora's Cave Publishing sells instantaneous downloads twenty-four hours a day, seven days a week, every day of the year. Our webstore is never closed. Our e-book delivery system is 100% automated, meaning your order is filled as soon as you pay for it.

Those are a few of the top reasons why electronic books are replacing paperbacks for many avid readers.

As always, Ellora's Cave and Cerridwen Press welcome your questions and comments. We invite you to email us at Comments@ellorascave.com or write to us directly at Ellora's Cave Publishing Inc., 1056 Home Avenue, Akron, OH 44310-3502.

Cerridwen Press

Cerridwen, the Celtic goddess of wisdom, was the muse who brought inspiration to storytellers and those in the creative arts.

Cerridwen Press encompasses the best and most innovative stories in all genres of today's fiction.

Visit our website and discover the newest titles by talented authors who still get inspired — much like the ancient storytellers did...

once upon a time.

www.cerridwenpress.com